JUDITH
LENNOX
The Turning Point

headline
review

First published in 2012 by HEADLINE REVIEW
An imprint of HEADLINE PUBLISHING GROUP

First published in paperback in 2013 by HEADLINE REVIEW

1

ISBN 978 0 7553 8410 5

Typeset in Joanna MT by Palimpsest Book Production Limited,
Falkirk, Stirlingshire

Printed and bound by
CPI Group (UK) Ltd, Croydon, CR0 4YY

Headline's policy is to use papers that are natural, renewable and recyclable
products and made from wood grown in sustainable forests. The logging
and manufacturing processes are expected to conform to the
environmental regulations of the country of origin.

HEADLINE PUBLISHING GROUP
An Hachette UK Company
338 Euston Road
London NW1 3BH

www.headline.co.uk
www.hachette.co.uk

To Marianne Elizabeth Smith

Acknowledgements

Thanks to my agent, Maggie Hanbury, my editor at Headline, Clare Foss, and my editor at Piper, Bettina Feldweg, for their support during the writing of this novel. Thanks, as always, are due to my family, especially my son, Dominic, for his help with the scientific parts of the book, and my husband, Iain, without whom my computer would not work and travel would be far less enjoyable.

Seil is a beautiful island off the west coast of Scotland. My thanks to the charming and welcoming owner of our B & B and to the many islanders who extended to us their warm hospitality.

Part One

Gildersleve

1952

Chapter One

It was the first cold morning of September.

A narrow lane angled sharply away from the main road, heading through a hazel wood. The chill autumn air was redolent of beginnings, of new academic years, something to get your teeth into after the torpor of late summer. A few leaves cast themselves adrift from the branches, scattering the verges with splashes of gold and crimson.

So you're going to be one of Pharoah's men. The remark, made to her by an academic acquaintance shortly after her interview six weeks ago, came back to Ellen Kingsley as she cycled up the incline. In her memory, the words were tinged with amusement and perhaps condescension. She had replied, 'I'm going to work at Gildersleve Hall, if that's what you mean,' and had felt a thrill of pleasure in saying so.

At the top of the rise she braked and looked out over

the shallow valley. The hedgerow and trees had fallen away and the fields were shaken out before her like a gold and brown quilt over the gently rolling landscape. A small grey tractor was ploughing up stubble. A flock of white birds wheeled in the blue sky before alighting on twists of earth.

Beyond the fields lay Gildersleve Hall, solid and uncompromising against this modest countryside. Half a dozen white poplars, their leafy heads shimmering silver in the breeze, stood beside the hall, and a line of cypress trees curved towards the road. A tower, wreathed in ivy, protruded from one side of the building. The heavy eaves over the two prominent bay windows gave the house the appearance of frowning, and the red-brick walls and slate roofs seemed to absorb the autumn sunshine. The house looked secretive, almost menacing, and if Ellen had believed in ghosts, she might have imagined it to be haunted.

But there was always an explanation for everything, and she knew that the heavy Victorian Gothic architecture lent itself to associations of mystery and the supernatural, and that the windows appeared blank because the scientists working in the laboratories would have put down the blinds to shut out the glare of the sun. And the flicker of apprehension she felt was caused by her excitement at this, her first day in a new job.

This was the opportunity she had worked for and longed for. This was the start of her future.

* * *

The lab in which she would grow her crystals was on the topmost floor of Gildersleve Hall.

On her arrival, a secretary had let her in, and a man of around Ellen's own age, pausing in the act of dashing upstairs, had looked back over his shoulder and said, 'You must be the new research assistant.' Introducing himself as Martin Finch, he offered to show her up to her lab. Climbing up flights of stairs, Ellen glimpsed offices and laboratories. A tall, dark-haired man hurried past them, acknowledging their presence with a nod and a word of greeting.

Martin had a plain, rather rubbery face, with a long, bulbous nose, full mouth and thick, black eyebrows. His tweed jacket was open over a jersey, shirt and tie. He wore his short brown hair parted to one side, and a spatulate fingertip jabbed at the bridge of his tortoiseshell glasses, which kept slipping down his nose.

He opened a door for her. 'These rooms are always freezing in winter,' he said. 'But you'll have your burning passion for science to keep you warm.'

That, and several jerseys, Ellen thought. A cold draught whistled through the small room. Two of the walls were lined with benches, on which stood microscopes, bunsen burners and retort stands. Two desks, the surface of one bare except for a lamp and inkwell, the other heaped with papers, pens, log books and slide rule, had been placed back to back in the centre of the room. A black metal filing cabinet squeezed into a corner, and books and box files were stacked on shelves. There was a calendar, the months written in French, pinned to a wall.

Ellen said, 'My last lab wasn't exactly luxurious, Dr Finch. Four of us in a space the size of a broom cupboard and a bomb crater outside the door.'

'You must call me Martin, Miss Kingsley. And I'm not Dr Finch, I'm a mere mister. Shall I tell you about the others?'

'Please.'

'There are two groups of scientists who work at Gildersleve Hall. Alpha and beta, I call them.'

'Who's alpha?'

'We are, of course. There's fewer of us, but we're cleverer. We're the protein group. The phage group – the betas – are in the other side of the house. There's about twenty of us scientists, as well as various other bods – technicians and secretaries, that sort of thing. You'll be sharing this lab with Mam'zelle.'

'Mam'zelle?'

'Andrée Fournier. We call her Mam'zelle. Quiet type. French. She has a cubbyhole where she brews her coffee. No men allowed in there on pain of death. She's been here about a year. She arrived a few weeks after me, does something clever with myoglobin molecules. Some of the older men have been here much longer. Who interviewed you?'

'Dr Kaminski.'

'He's been at Gildersleve for donkey's years. He joined

in the war when the hall was doing all the top-secret stuff. He's a Pole, clever bloke, was in the RAF then got shot up rather and ended up here.'

At her interview, Ellen had seen that one side of Dr Kaminski's face was a mass of scar tissue, the legacy, she assumed, of his wartime career. It had been hard to look at him without flinching and without pity.

Martin went on, 'Kaminski's Pharoah's deputy, fills in for him when he's away on one of his jaunts. Pharoah's at a conference in America just now, so Kaminski's top dog. Padfield and Farmborough are old-timers as well, ex-army types. Padfield's a first-rate batsman, captains the cricket team. We have a few matches against some of the Cambridge labs in the summer, it's jolly good fun. But I don't suppose you're interested in cricket, Ellen.'

She smiled. 'My brother's very keen, so I've learned to take an interest.'

'Padfield and Farmborough are chemists, crystallographers. You'll be making your crystals for them, as well as for Jan Kaminski. Toby Dorner works on this floor too. He's a biochemist, Jewish, came over here from Austria in the thirties, when he was just a kid.'

'And the man who passed us as we came upstairs? The tall, dark man?'

'Jock, you mean? His name's Alec Hunter, but we all call him Jock.'

'Scottish, then?'

'Very well deduced.'

She could not tell whether he was being sarcastic or not.

'I think you'll find our group's a friendly bunch,' added Martin. 'Apart from Dr Redmond, of course. He was here in the war too. Farmborough once told me he was senior to Pharoah back then. He's an odd chap.'

'Why do you say that?'

He went to the window. 'That's his cottage.'

Ellen looked out. The window looked down to the area of land behind Gildersleve Hall. There were several outhouses, including the shed in which she had put her bike. Beyond were the tall poplars she had glimpsed earlier from the road; behind them, ploughed fields and hedgerows. Following Martin's pointing finger to the skyline, Ellen caught sight of a cottage, standing beside woodland.

'It's in the middle of nowhere,' he said. 'But that's how Redmond likes it, the miserable blighter. His lab's in the tower. Gets in a huff if you go in there.'

'Perhaps he dislikes being interrupted.'

'Perhaps he doesn't care for company. I don't think he has a friend in the world.'

'Is he married?'

Finch guffawed. 'Good Lord, no. Padfield and Farmborough have wives and families. The rest of our group are footloose and fancy free.' He had taken off his glasses and was polishing them with his tie. Uncovered, Ellen noticed a sharpness in his eyes.

'Do you come from round here?' he asked.

'I'm from all over the place. My father's in the army. I went to Bristol University.'

'Hah, red-brick like me, then. Where are you lodging?'

'In Copfield. It seemed most convenient, only three miles on the bike.'

'There's a pretty decent pub in Copfield, the Green Man.' Martin put his glasses back on and blinked. 'Some of us sometimes have a drink there after work. You should join us – as I said, we're a friendly bunch.'

The door opened and Martin Finch broke off. A small, slender woman, her glossy dark hair neatly pinned up at the back of her head and her clothing hidden under a white lab coat, came into the room. She was carrying a coffee cup, covered by a saucer. Putting it down on the bench, she said, 'Hello, Martin.' And to Ellen, 'You must be Miss Kingsley. I'm Andrée Fournier.'

The two women shook hands. Then Miss Fournier said, 'Thank you, Martin. I can show Miss Kingsley where everything is,' and Martin left the lab.

Andrée Fournier was strikingly pretty. Her face was heart-shaped and her complexion was flawless and golden. She had emphasized her dark-brown eyes with a light application of liner and mascara and she wore a neat navy-blue skirt and jersey.

'Would you like a coffee, Miss Kingsley?' she asked. 'There's some in the pot.'

'Please.'

'Come with me. I'll show you where you may put your coat.'

Across the landing, Miss Fournier opened a door. This room was very small, little wider than a corridor. A small, high, narrow window framed an oblong of sky and there was an unshaded electric light bulb, a sink and a kettle. Above the sink was a mirror; to its side were coat pegs, on one of which hung a red woollen scarf and a grey coat.

Ellen hung her coat on the second hook and breathed in the aroma of coffee. 'What a gorgeous smell.'

'The coffee the others drink is vile. My mother sends me the beans from France.' There was a coffee pot beside the kettle; Andrée poured out a cup.

Ellen said, 'Martin seems very friendly.'

'Ah, yes. Though these men, and their silly names for people . . . Martin can be such a child. Help yourself to sugar.'

'I suppose nicknames can be rather tiresome.'

'You will be "Ginger", Miss Kingsley. It's inevitable.' Miss Fournier's voice was dry.

Ellen smiled. 'I was "Ginger" all the way through school and college, so I'm used to it. "Carrot-top" was worse.'

'You have beautiful hair. I used to long to have auburn hair like yours when I was a little girl.'

The coffee was delicious, rich and stimulating. Ellen asked, 'What do you do for lunch? I wasn't sure so I brought sandwiches.'

'Dr Padfield and Dr Farmborough often go home for

lunch, but most of us have sandwiches in the common room. There's a fire there, so it's warm in winter, but sometimes I prefer to come up here. The common room can be so noisy. Miriam cooks for Dr Pharoah and Dr Kaminski. When the men eat in the dining room, she cooks for them too.'

'Only the men?'

'Women aren't allowed in the dining room. It's a tradition. The others eat there when we have a visitor.'

There was a tonelessness in Miss Fournier's conversation, which Ellen put down to the difficulty of speaking in a foreign language. She said, 'Which part of France do you come from?'

A flicker of animation on Andrée Fournier's perfect features. 'Paris. Do you know it?'

'A little. I spent a week there last year. The university arranged it. It was wonderful – such a beautiful city. You must miss it.'

'Yes, I do.' Miss Fournier glanced at her watch. 'It's a quarter to nine. We should get to work.'

At one o'clock, Ellen and Andrée went downstairs to the common room. It was furnished with an electric fire, armchairs and occasional tables, as well as some hard chairs and stools. A large bay window looked out on to the gravel courtyard at the front of the house. There was an air of mild disorder: on the tabletops, apple cores and biscuit wrappings were mixed in with pens, ashtrays, newspapers and periodicals. A record player was playing a Rosemary Clooney song and the room smelled of pipe smoke and instant coffee.

Andrée sat down on a stool and began to unwrap her sandwiches. Ellen sat beside her.

'Well, well, the new recruit to our merry band!' A big, red-faced man put down his newspaper and crossed the room, offering his hand to Ellen. 'Farmborough, Bill Farmborough. Welcome to Gildersleve Hall, Miss Kingsley.'

'Thank you.' She shook his hand.

'I'll do the honours, shall I? That oaf in the corner is Denis Padfield.' There was a wave and a grunt from a balding man in a herringbone tweed jacket. 'You've met Finch, haven't you? And this is Toby Dorner. Put down that foul brew you've made, Bat, and say hello to the nice lady.'

Toby Dorner was young, short and slight, with close-cropped, curly brown hair and protruding ears, which gave him an impish look. Standing up, he took Ellen's hand. 'It's a pleasure to meet you, Miss Kingsley,' he said. 'I'm delighted that you're joining us.' His voice was gently accented.

Someone stuck his head round the common-room door. Ellen recognized him as the dark-haired man she had encountered on the stairs earlier that day, Alec Hunter.

Bill Farmborough said, 'Come and meet Miss Kingsley, Jock.'

Hunter introduced himself to Ellen, shaking her hand. He had a distracted air, as if his attention was elsewhere.

12

He made a quick gesture with the papers he was holding, saying, 'Kaminsky wanted these in a hurry. Any idea where he is?'

'Last time I saw him he was heading for the tower.'

'Thanks. Excuse me, Miss Kingsley.' Dr Hunter left the room.

In Alec Hunter's absence, the memory of his appearance – clear brow, almond-shaped dark blue eyes, a firm, well-shaped mouth, aquiline nose and tousled dark hair – lingered, like the after-image of a bright light.

A discussion about her lodgings followed; Ellen was fortunate in finding a room with Mrs Bryant, someone said, and horror stories were told about other digs in the area.

'Bat's frightfully energetic,' drawled Martin. 'Cycles come rain or shine. Me, I'm a lazy blighter and I drive a car.'

'It's not a *car*, Miss Kingsley,' said Denis Padfield. 'It's a rust heap. When it rains, pieces fall off it.'

Martin crumpled a sheet of newspaper into a ball and hurled it at Padfield. Andrée rose to her feet and left the room.

Padfield sighed. 'See now, Finch, you've gone and put Mam'zelle into a huff. Now she'll be ratty with us all.'

Ellen said, 'Why do they call you Bat, Dr Dorner?'

'Looks like a bat, don't you think? Skinny . . . big ears . . .'

'It's because he can find his way in the dark,' explained Martin. 'Whenever there's a blackout, Bat flits happily about while the rest of us are falling over our feet.'

'Are there often blackouts?'

'Now and then. This house has its own electricity generator.'

An electric kettle stood on a table near the window; the shelves above it held mugs and tea and coffee. Ellen asked whether anyone wanted a drink; Denis Padfield asked for a cup of tea. She took down two mugs from the shelf.

Bill Farmborough drawled, 'Not the striped one, it's Redmond's. Gets into a frightful bate if anyone else uses his mug.'

Ellen put back the striped mug and took down a plain one instead. They were all pleasant and friendly, she thought, though she understood why they irritated Andrée Fournier. She herself was used to schoolboyish banter: her brother, Joe, was four years younger than she was.

An older man came into the room. He was of average build but stooped, so that his gaze directed downwards. His ill-cut grey hair had thinned on top and he was wearing National Health spectacles. His clothing looked worn and not at all clean. Over an off-white shirt he wore a baggy brown corduroy jacket with leather elbow patches that were cracked and fraying.

Toby Dorner said, 'Hello, Redmond,' but the older man did not respond. He crossed the room to the table with the tea things, took down the striped mug and spooned in tea. When the kettle boiled, he poured water on to the leaves and gave the mug a vigorous stir.

'Good morning, Dr Redmond,' said Ellen, and introduced herself.

He was standing only a couple of feet away from her but he did not respond, did not even look at her. She might have been invisible. She might not have existed.

Once he had made his tea, Dr Redmond left the room, mug in hand. Dr Padfield called after him, 'And nice to talk to you too, Redmond!' and there was a murmur of laughter.

Then Bill Farmborough said, 'Pharoah, I didn't think we'd see you till the end of the week,' and immediately everyone fell silent, as if a switch had been flicked.

It was Ellen's first glimpse of the director of Gildersleve Hall, Marcus Pharoah. His tall, broad-shouldered form was flattered by a beautifully cut charcoal-grey suit. The collar of his white shirt was crisp and the silk of his tie was elegantly striped in muted shades of maroon and gold. Pharoah's features were regular and handsome, a few silver strands showing through his black hair. He held himself easily, the stance of a man used to commanding the attention of a room.

'Good morning, gentlemen. And good morning, ladies.' His dark brown eyes came to rest on Ellen. 'You must be Miss Kingsley.'

Dr Pharoah welcomed Ellen to Gildersleve, apologizing for having been too busy to greet her earlier. 'Have my troops been looking after you, Miss Kingsley?'

'Yes, thank you, very well.'

'I'm pleased to hear it. Let me tell you what I wanted to make of the hall. I wanted to create a laboratory in which I could mix all the disciplines together. Biochemists, molecular biologists, physicists, chemists, crystallographers . . . perhaps even a mathematician or two. I wanted to make an environment where new ideas might meld together and find a receptive audience. Other institutions − King's and the Cavendish, for instance − strive for the same, but I like to think we've managed it rather better. Some of our visitors tell me they find the atmosphere at Gildersleve Hall rather frantic, but I like that. I doubt if great ideas come out of monastic silences. I believe they're more likely to develop from a mixing pot, even if the bubbling and brewing makes a bit of a racket.'

There was a silence. Ellen wondered whether anyone else in the room was having to fight the desire to applaud.

Bill Farmborough spoke. 'How was America, Pharoah?'

'Useful, very useful. But we must be on our mettle, gentlemen − the race is to the swift.' Dr Pharoah smiled. 'And if no one offers me a cup of tea soon, I shall desiccate.'

'We wouldn't want that. Our lord and master reduced to a heap of powder.' Farmborough put on the kettle.

A discussion followed about the lines of research being undertaken at the hall. Opinions were batted back and forth, suppositions confronted and taken apart with surgical precision. Then Marcus Pharoah made his apologies and left the room.

Ellen ate her lunch. Bill Farmborough went back to his newspaper, a chess game started up, and Rosemary Clooney sang, her voice like honey, 'If you loved me half as much as I loved you.'

She was a Daddy's girl, she supposed. Her father, who was a Royal Engineer, had always delighted in her faculty for maths and science. He had shown her how to take apart a motorcycle engine and put it together again and they had stood together in the frosty darkness of Salisbury Plain, watching a meteorite shower. Though winning a prize at school had been important to her, winning her father's approval had mattered far more.

Her childhood had been one of new houses, new schools, different places and different people as the family had moved between army camps. She had acquired the ability to remember people's names and to fit in anywhere. At the age of twelve she had been sent to boarding school in Buckinghamshire. She had enjoyed school, which had provided her with an anchor, especially during wartime. A teacher had encouraged her talent for science; after leaving school she had taken a degree in chemistry at Bristol University, followed by a year's research. She had known by then that she was no theoretician, that her gifts were technical, for experimentation, where her methodical, careful intelligence, her powers of observation and her determination to discover the truth and to prove it as far as possible beyond doubt were assets.

17

Her final-year project at Bristol had been on crystallography. The growing of crystals was something she had found she had a knack for, which was why she had been offered the job of research assistant at Gildersleve Hall. This was how she would spend her days: investigating those tiny, beautiful, slivers of perfection.

A short, burly man in a camouflage jacket, a brindled bull terrier at his heels, was coming away from the outhouses when, at the end of the afternoon, Ellen went to collect her bicycle. She said good evening and he gave her a sharp look and then a curt nod.

She took her bicycle out of the shed and wheeled it to the gravelled forecourt in front of the hall. Martin was loading cardboard boxes into a small Austin parked there.

'You look rather heavily laden,' she said.

Martin looked up. He was red-faced and a line of sweat darkened the hair on his forehead. 'They weigh a ton. Have you survived your first day?'

She laughed. 'Just about.'

'I hated it at first. I felt like a new boy at school. I wanted to turn tail and run.' He glanced at the boxes. 'I'd offer you a lift but I have to take these to Mrs Pharoah. She's some charity do on.'

The lid of one of the boxes flapped open, revealing a stack of plates. Ellen said, 'It's all right, thanks, I've got the bike.'

Martin lifted a box on to the front seat of the car. 'I

18

thought I might call in to the jolly old Green Man tonight. Some of the others said they'd come. If you don't mind my prattle, you could always join us.'

'Thank you,' she murmured, then she said goodbye and cycled away.

Her lodgings were in a bungalow on a road that struck out from Copfield towards Cambridge. Her landlady, Mrs Bryant, was a war widow in her early thirties. Mrs Bryant had one child, a twelve-year-old daughter, Gillian. The three of them ate supper together and afterwards Ellen retired to her room, where she wrote a letter to her parents and another to her boyfriend, Daniel Risborough.

Daniel lived in London, where he shared a flat in Marble Arch with his elder brother Clarence. He was a linguist and worked for the Diplomatic Service. They had met ten months ago, on a train – or, rather, they had met just after they had left the train, because Daniel had forgotten his umbrella and Ellen had run after him with it. He had offered to buy her a drink. 'I was trying to think how to ask you out,' he said to her, 'but I couldn't work out how to do it, but now I can, to thank you for returning my umbrella.' Since then, they had met up when the opportunity arose. She went with Daniel to concerts and art galleries, and sometimes they kissed, and now and then tentative suggestions of engagement and marriage were voiced and then put aside.

In her letter, Ellen described her first day at Gildersleve Hall, emphasizing the parts that she thought might interest

Daniel: the architecture of the hall and the laboratory's connections with Cambridge (Daniel was a Trinity man). She finished by reminding him of their arrangement to meet for lunch in October (the forgetfulness with the umbrella had not been an isolated incident). Then she left the bungalow to post her letters.

The light was fading as she walked down the road and crossed the village green to a Norman church with its square central tower. The dying sun gilded the flints and stones of the ancient walls. The postbox was at the end of a winding lane overhung by hawthorns, the box itself almost lost beneath the foliage. Beyond the end of the lane was a disused RAF aerodrome, to one side of which was a new council estate, built to house the families who had come from the bombed cities to live in the Nissen huts after the end of the war.

Ellen continued her circuit of the village, eventually striking back towards its heart. The Green Man pub, which stood beside the village green, had a grey and mossy thatched roof. Remembering Martin's invitation, she went inside.

Two couples sat in the private bar, sipping their drinks in genteel silence. Noise issued from the public bar, swelling as Ellen opened the door. The room was crowded. Men turned to stare at her, their gazes running from her head to her toes. A quick scan told her that, apart from the barmaid, she was the only woman in the room.

Martin was sitting at a corner table. She waved to him.

'Ellen!' He rose to his feet. 'You don't mind sitting here, do you? The saloon bar's as dead as a mortuary. Let me get you a drink. What would you like?'

'A half of bitter, please.'

She sat down at the table. When Martin came back with the drinks she asked after the others.

'Looks like they couldn't make it. Cheers.' He chinked his glass against hers. 'I didn't think you were going to come. I saw you earlier, walking across the green.'

'I had letters to post, and,' she lowered her voice, 'my room is perfectly comfortable but there are about half a dozen different patterns in it. Curtains, eiderdown, carpet, rug . . . it's a little oppressive.' She smiled. 'My boyfriend would find it unbearable. He would have moved out by now – either that or had a nervous breakdown.'

'Boyfriend?' said Martin.

'Daniel lives in London.'

'Ah.'

'When I was leaving the hall this afternoon, I saw a man at the outhouses. Tough-looking . . . wearing an army jacket. He wasn't particularly friendly.'

'That would have been Gosse.' Martin grimaced. 'Pharoah's familiar.'

'Why do you call him that?'

'Gosse has been the janitor at Gildersleve Hall since it was first set up.' Martin cast a glance round the room. 'Just checking. He drinks here sometimes. Pharoah met him during the war. Rumour is, Roy Gosse was just out of

21

military prison and Pharoah got him transferred here. Gosse's obnoxious to the rest of us but would do anything for Pharoah. He's useful, I'll give him that. Keeps the old place running, fixes the boiler and defrosts the pipes in the middle of winter, that sort of thing.'

'You sound as though you dislike him.'

Martin shrugged. 'I don't care about him one way or the other. I wouldn't cross him, that's for sure. He has a nasty temper. Keep-fit fanatic, used to be a boxer, apparently.' He offered Ellen a cigarette; she thanked him but declined.

He said, 'What did you think of us all, then?'

'Everyone was very kind and helpful.'

'*Everyone*? Come off it, Kingsley.' Martin flicked a lighter. 'Redmond? *Helpful*?'

'Perhaps not him. Actually, I felt sorry for him.'

'Why? He's an unfriendly devil.'

'He looked . . . uncared-for. And perhaps he's shy, rather than unfriendly.'

'Why on earth should he feel shy? He just can't be bothered, and that's the truth of it. Thinks the rest of us are beneath him.'

She did not argue the point further. Martin said, 'And Mam'zelle? Do you think you're going to like sharing a lab with her?'

'Yes, I would have thought so.'

'She's got a sharp tongue, you know. Mind you, Hunter tends to get the worst of it these days.'

'Does Andrée dislike him?'

'She used to *adore* him.' Martin rolled his eyes. 'Madly, passionately, you know, and then it all fell apart. Now, when they're in the same room together you can cut the atmosphere with a knife.'

'That's the trouble with workplace romances. If it all ends badly you still have to see each other every day.'

'I get on with Jock, on the whole, but he's lord of the manor or some such back home, and he can be a moody devil. And Mam'zelle blows hot and cold. I expect they bickered like cat and dog.'

At their meeting in the common room that morning Dr Hunter's dark blue eyes had rested on her for a moment without a flicker of a smile and had then slid aside. Ellen knew that her attraction to him was not real, that it was some transference of the hope and excitement she had invested in her new job. He was a handsome man, undeniably, but once you got to know someone, as a colleague or a friend, handsomeness was as easily forgotten as ugliness.

Martin said, 'What did you think of Pharoah's speech this morning? You know,' he put on a pompous voice, 'creating a laboratory in which all the disciplines are mixed together . . . great ideas . . .'

'I thought it was inspiring.'

'I suppose it is if you haven't heard it before.' Martin fidgeted with a beer mat. 'He adds a new bit now and then, for neophytes like you.'

'Has Dr Pharoah a family?'

'A wife, Alison, and a daughter, Rowena. They live in Barton. Alison's rather a bitch. I suppose I shouldn't say that, but it's true. Her family's very rich and she looks down on lesser folk. I think that to begin with, just after the war, the Pharoahs lived in the hall itself. Probably wasn't grand enough for Alison, so they bought the house in Barton.' Martin grinned. 'My landlady tells me there are ghosts at Gildersleve Hall.'

'Ghosts?'

'A child, a little boy, died in the house, fell downstairs or something. You're supposed to be able to hear his footsteps at night, running up and down the corridors. Creepy.' Martin made spooky movements with his hands. 'Bat has this idea that you can explain the sighting of ghosts using quantum theory.'

Ellen laughed. 'A fanciful imagination seems more likely.'

'Or a drink too many.' Martin glanced at her empty glass. 'Can I get you another?'

She shook her head. 'Thanks, Martin, but I won't. I should get back to my digs. I'm rather tired – it's been a long day.'

'I'll give you a lift.'

'There's no need. It's no distance.'

'Save you the walk.' He stood up, shrugging on his jacket.

On alternate Monday afternoons, a seminar was given by a staff member of Dr Pharoah's choosing to the entire group. 'So who's to be skewered over the hot coals today?' murmured Martin, sliding into the seat beside Ellen. She tried to imagine what it must feel like, to know that Dr Pharoah had chosen you to present your work to the group. She listened attentively to the discussions and noted her colleagues' differing contributions. Bill Farmborough deferred to Pharoah while Denis Padfield found fault with everything. Toby was pithy and incisive, but Martin's interjections, in which his words often fell over each other in his rush to make his point, were sometimes brilliant but at other times misplaced. As for Alec Hunter, Ellen noticed that for much of the time he was silent. Now and then, with an air of scowling impatience, he would lean forward and make some remark, sometimes cutting, but sometimes, she was forced to admit, shrewd. She found herself disliking him for his air of holding himself apart from other people; she wondered whether he considered his opinions too precious to be shared. And yet the attraction she had felt for him had not completely gone away but would sometimes catch her by surprise, powerful and disturbing.

Now and then, flicking through The Times or Nature, she saw Dr Pharoah's name. Funny, that, to know someone who existed in another, more celebrated world. It was almost as if a little of the magic might rub off on her. One evening, Ellen and Mrs Bryant sat in Mrs Bryant's living room, listening to Dr Pharoah give a talk on the Third Programme. Ellen was sewing on buttons and Mrs Bryant was knitting. The tip-tap of needles and the rasp of thread through the cloth, and Dr Pharoah's good-for-radio voice, murmuring of genes and proteins: like coming across a Monet in a public library, too important and cultured for the small room, with its lemon-washed anaglypta wallpaper, plump, beribboned cushions and china cats.

Marcus Pharoah was clever and amusing and commanding. But there was something else, some extra dash of an ingredient Ellen could not find the words for, some rare element or catalyst that by its presence transformed. When Dr Pharoah joined them in the common room, the air seemed charged with electricity and their discussions were whipped into life. After he had gone, they were, according to their natures, exhausted or exhilarated or fractious, each of them, Ellen suspected, rerunning the conversation in their heads, trying to judge whether they had acquitted themselves well.

'The gods have come down from Olympus,' Martin muttered to her, one Monday afternoon when Marcus Pharoah and a colleague from the Cavendish joined the regular seminar. An obvious metaphor, but Ellen could see what he meant.

She was preparing a batch of crystals for Jan Kaminski, when, from a distance, she heard raised voices. At first she disregarded them, returning her mind to the quiet, empty place that allowed her to work best. But they rose in volume, and eventually she went out to the landing. The voices were coming from the tower. One belonged to Marcus Pharoah;

she assumed that the other was Dr Redmond's. She could not make out any words, only the unpleasant angular rise and fall of the argument.

She was poised like an eavesdropper: she went back into the lab and shut the door. She heard one of the men leave the tower, his footsteps fast and clipped. Dr Pharoah, she thought – Dr Redmond shuffled as he walked, scuffing his feet. She focused her attention on making a tiny wire cage, twisting the wire so that it was exactly the right size to contain the crystal she would place inside it. A door slammed. More footsteps, then a loud clang, as if someone had stumbled against something.

After a while, checking her watch, Ellen saw that it was lunchtime and left the lab. In the corridor, her eye was caught by a scattering of sand from the fire bucket. Something was inside the bucket; she took it out. It was an Osmiroid fountain pen, tortoiseshell with a gilt cap. Her thumb grazed against a roughness on the barrel and she read the name engraved there: B. D. J. Redmond. Dr Redmond must have tripped over the fire bucket and dropped his pen.

She felt reluctant to enter the tower, knowing that she was crossing a boundary. It was quieter there than in the rest of the building, colder too, because three of the walls were exposed to the elements. On the open landing were bookshelves, bowed beneath the weight of dusty, browning periodicals.

'Dr Redmond?' she called out, but there was no reply. Even if Dr Redmond had gone back to his lab, would he answer her? During the four weeks she had been working at Gildersleve Hall, he had not spoken to her once.

She went upstairs. On the upper landing, she tapped on a door, then went inside the lab. Cluttered, you might have said, except the word in no way did justice to the accumulation of books, journals and scientific equipment there. The only light was from a tall, narrow window which looked out to the garden and copse. Through it, Ellen saw Dr Redmond standing beneath the trees, looking up with a pair of binoculars into the branches.

She returned downstairs, took her coat from the box room and went outside. The air was cool and fresh, gusts of wind shaking the bare branches of the poplars.

She called out, 'Hello, Dr Redmond!' and he turned to her.

'I brought you this.' She held out the pen. 'You dropped it in the fire bucket.'

His hand went to his jacket pocket, patting it flat. He took the pen from her.

She said, 'Have you seen anything interesting?'

'A mistle thrush.' He looked up at the sky, blinking. His eyes were large and pale blue, fringed with light-coloured lashes. 'There's always been a mistle thrush in this copse,' he said. 'Even when they cut the trees down, the mistle thrush stayed.'

'Which trees?'

'Down there.' He gestured towards the field that butted up to the perimeter of the copse. 'Before the war, these woods were twice the size. Sheer vandalism – a waste of effort as well as the pointless destruction of an ancient woodland. The ground's always been boggy. No crops have ever grown there.'

'Still, it's pretty.'

'It doesn't compare to Peddar's Wood for birds. I go there every day. I always see something.'

'How marvellous,' she said, but some movement in the upper branches had caught his attention and he had lost interest in the conversation. Turning away from her, he raised the binoculars again.

Then a brindled bull terrier rushed through the under-growth towards them. There was a beating of wings and Dr Redmond flinched and took a step back.

'Gosse should keep that dog under control,' he muttered. Putting his head down, he walked away down the path.

The next day was a Saturday. Ellen caught the train from Cambridge to meet Daniel. Alighting at King's Cross Station, she caught sight of Dr Redmond ahead of her on the plat-form, among the passengers spilling out of the train. After a few moments he disappeared into the crowds heading for the Underground station.

Daniel was waiting for her by the barrier. He kissed her cheek and asked after her journey. Then they took an Underground train to Leicester Square, to visit the National Gallery. On the train, she asked him about his work and he said, 'I've been very busy. I've worked late each night this week,' and jabbed at his fringe to brush it out of his eyes.

'Poor Daniel, you must be exhausted.'

'I don't mind the extra work, but there was a concert I wanted to go to, and I had to give the tickets to Clarence.'

Inside the National Gallery, they looked at the Titians, Daniel's favourites. Daniel disliked the modern, his lack of enthusiasm extending to the nineteenth century, though he admitted a grudging admiration for Turner and Pissarro. Ellen had once said exasperatedly to him, 'Daniel, you can't just dismiss every single twentieth-century artist,' and he had turned to her, puzzlement in his great blue eyes, and said, 'But Ellen, "Diana and Actaeon" and a Jackson Pollock – how can you even *compare* them?'

He was very knowledgeable, and she had always tolerated – often enjoyed – his habit of giving lectures on each painting, but today her thoughts swung away to Gildersleve Hall, even while her gaze was fixed on the swirling draperies and contorted limbs of 'Bacchus and Ariadne'. It felt strange to pick up the strands of her previous life. She felt rusty, ill at ease, almost as if she was taking a step back.

Daniel finished speaking of brushstrokes and Titian's use of colour. Ellen said, 'It's always surprised me that "Bacchus and Ariadne" should be one of your favourites. It's so wild and forceful.'

He gave a patient smile. 'No, Ellen, you're missing the point. The painting may *appear* wild and forceful, but the composition is magnificently controlled.'

'The composition's only a means to an end, a technique for conveying whatever it is that the artist wants to say.' She studied the painted figure of Bacchus, the angle of his shoulders, the tension in his muscles and the desire in the gaze that focused on the fleeing Ariadne. 'Just look at the expressions on their faces. There's such darkness there!'

'I don't see why you should be surprised that I admire it.'

'Like it, Daniel, or love it,' she said impatiently. 'It's more than mere admiration, surely?'

He hunched his shoulders. 'I prefer not to speak of art in woolly emotional terms.'

'That's exactly what I mean. You talk in such a measured way, and yet you enjoy art that's full of desire and hunger and fear.'

They walked out of the room in silence. Their disagreement had blown up out of nowhere – they had never quarrelled before and it dismayed her. What was wrong with her? His face was set; she felt a pang of guilt and squeezed his hand.

They left the gallery shortly afterwards and lunched in a small French restaurant in the Strand. Tables were dotted round a square room whose window looked out on to a courtyard garden. One fine evening the previous summer they had dined in the garden, though Daniel had disliked the wasps.

Daniel ordered steak and potatoes and Ellen asked for an omelette and salad. When their food arrived, Daniel carefully separated the potatoes from the steak, a habit which Ellen had once found endearing but today thought childish.

He said suddenly, 'I've been offered a post in Paris.'

'*Paris!*' She looked up at him. 'Daniel, why didn't you say?'

'I didn't feel there was the opportunity.'

'How exciting! I'm so pleased for you.'

He looked puzzled. 'I was always convinced that when I was finally posted abroad, it would be to somewhere bleak and uncivilized. Or crashingly dull, perhaps.'

'You will go, won't you?'

'Yes, I think so.'

'I'll come and visit you.'

'Will you, Ellen?'

Something in his tone made her reach across the table and take his hand. 'Yes, of course.'

'I wondered whether to ask you to come with me. In fact, I thought I might ask you to marry me.'

'Daniel—'

But before she could go on, he added, 'But I don't think it would work.'

It was irrational, she knew, that she should feel irked that he should dismiss her so easily when she would have refused him anyway. 'Oh,' she said coldly. 'I see.'

'I think that place has changed you.'

'*Changed* me?' She gave him a hard look. 'I don't suppose you mean for the better.'

32

'I didn't say that. I just meant that you seem different. You seem,' he pursed his mouth, '*distracted*.'

'It's my first proper job. It's important to me. You don't mind, do you?'

'Mind? Why should I mind?'

'I don't know, Daniel. You've hardly asked me about Gildersleve Hall.'

'We were at the gallery. I don't believe that's a place for chit-chat. Well then, how is it going?'

'It's fine. I think it's going to work out very well.' His brisk, humouring tone annoyed her. If she had told him how she really felt about working at Gildersleve Hall – proud, exhilarated, sometimes apprehensive – he would say something deflating, she suspected.

'I don't think you'd leave Gildersleve Hall for me, would you, Ellen?'

There was a long, difficult moment when neither of them spoke. Eventually he said, 'I don't want any pudding, do you?' and she shook her head.

Daniel paid the bill and they left the restaurant. One cold kiss and mutual expressions of good will, then he walked away while she headed in the opposite direction, for the Underground and the Islington lodgings that her brother Joe shared with half a dozen other students.

She found herself, later on that afternoon and over a cup of coffee in the kitchen, telling Joe about Daniel's proposal, feeling some guilt in doing so but needing to talk about it to someone, and if not her brother, then who else? Joe, who was cheerful and athletic and had yellow hair rather than red, hooted with laughter and said, 'I bet Risborough didn't fall on his knees and beg for your hand in marriage. I bet he said "it might be a jolly good idea if we got married" or something wishy-washy like that,' and she was forced to admit that yes, that was exactly what had happened.

'You said no, didn't you?'

'I didn't have to. He more or less said it himself.'

'Just as well. You'd have made mincemeat of the poor bloke, Ellie.'

'Honestly, I wouldn't at all. You make me sound like a harpy.' Yet she had a sudden, awful vision of how marriage to Daniel might have been, tepid and restrained and ultimately stifling.

She caught the half past seven train back to Cambridge. In the carriage, her attention drifted from her book and she looked out of the window, watching the countryside rush by. She felt unsettled and was glad to be returning to Copfield. *That place has changed you*, Daniel had said. Was that true? Surely it was rather that Gildersleve Hall had informed her, allowing her to see new possibilities. She was still Ellen, and her character, principles and ambitions remained the same. She did not believe that any place had the power to alter her in a fundamental way. But she felt low nevertheless, weary of the day and its events.

She left the train at Cambridge and caught a bus to Copfield. Leaving the bus, she shivered in the sharp, cold air. As she walked past the Green Man she glanced through

34

the window and saw Martin Finch. She had a yearning for uncomplicated friendship: she went inside.

Catching sight of her in the doorway, Martin rose to his feet. 'Evening, Kingsley. What'll you have?'

She asked for a beer, then took off her coat and sat down at the table. The room was full. The only other woman there was sitting at a high stool at the bar. She was middle-aged, a slash of red lipstick across her powdered face. She was wearing a Persian lamb jacket and a felt hat with a feather, and when she raised her glass to her mouth a chunky gold bracelet slid down her arm.

Martin came back with the drinks. He had been working that day, he told her – he liked being at Gildersleve when no one else was there. Well, only Gosse, and Redmond sometimes worked weekends, though he had not been in that day.

'I saw Dr Redmond on the London train,' Ellen told him.

Martin smiled. 'Good Lord – Redmond, going on a jaunt. Or maybe he has a secret life. How was London?'

'Not so good.' Her spirits collapsed like air out of a punctured tyre. 'I broke up with my boyfriend.' She could almost have cried, then and there, thinking of Daniel and the way they had parted.

Martin looked interested. 'That's rotten luck. You do need cheering up. I'll get you something stronger than that.'

Before Ellen could stop him, he rose and went to the bar, returning a few minutes later with a gin and tonic.

'Here, knock that back.'

'You're very sweet, Martin.'

He threw back his arms behind his head, stretching them, narrowly missing the head of the man sitting behind him. 'We aim to serve.'

'We weren't suited anyway. Daniel is very cultured.'

'You weren't in love with him, were you?'

Ellen considered that. 'No, I don't think so. He was very handsome and he was always very courteous, which I liked, and he had a knack of picking out the best, whatever it was. But I wasn't in love with him.' The gin had made her feel pleasantly fuzzy, otherwise she might not have added, 'I don't think I've ever been in love with anyone.'

She had had two boyfriends before Daniel. Giles had been in her year at Bristol, and then there had been Archie, who had been a junior doctor at the Royal Infirmary. She had lost her virginity to Archie, after a particularly wild party. Archie had been rather a mistake.

She lowered her voice, glancing at the bar. 'Sometimes I'm afraid I'll end up like *her*.'

Martin followed her gaze to the woman in the Persian lamb jacket, and sniggered. 'That old hag. I've seen her before, propping up the bar in here. Come off it.'

'How many of us are even dating anyone?'

'I think Toby has something going on with some woman in Cambridge. He's very cagey about it. And you can understand why Kaminski lives on his own, poor sod. As for Hunter, he's only got himself to blame. Women fall at his feet with sickening regularity.'

'Not Andrée.'

'Not any more, no.' His gaze settled on her. 'You're just choosing the wrong men, Kingsley.'

She laughed. 'Fall in love with another biochemist, you mean, and then perhaps we wouldn't end up quarrelling in the National Gallery.'

He laughed again, so hard he had to blow his nose and wipe his eyes. 'How middle-class you are.'

When they left the pub an hour later, a frost had begun to glisten on the road. Martin scraped a clear patch on the windscreen, then they drove out of the village. Ellen huddled in her coat, washed over by a feeling of pleasant detachment, as if much of what had occurred that day had happened to some other, quite distant person.

Martin parked the Austin outside Mrs Bryant's bungalow. 'Ellen,' he said.

'Yes, Martin?'

'I do like you a lot, you know.'

'And I'm terribly fond of you.'

'Are you cold?'

'A little.'

'Here, let me.' He reached over and put an arm round her. And then suddenly he was kissing her, his hand first squeezing her arm, then sliding beneath the folds of her coat.

She tried to say, 'Martin, don't,' but was hampered by his mouth, which was clamped wetly over her own, making it hard to breathe or speak, so in the end she gave him a shove. Then a harder shove, which startled him enough to draw back, allowing her to say, 'Martin, stop it.'

'But I thought—'

'What?'

'You're so beautiful! You must have realized how I feel about you!'

'Oh, Martin, don't be so silly!' The words snapped out of her.

His expression changed. 'Silly?'

'Yes,' she said crossly. She was annoyed with him for spoiling their evening. She opened the car door. 'You've had too much to drink. I'm going in now. I'll see you next week.'

There was an envelope on Ellen's desk when she arrived at the lab on Monday morning. She opened it and read the note inside. It was from Dr Pharoah, inviting her to Sunday lunch at his home in Barton.

She had hoped that Martin would have forgotten Saturday's embarrassing tussle in the car, but in the common room at break time, he bent over the parts of the Austin's starter motor, which he had spread out on a sheet of newspaper, and acknowledged her presence with only a grunt. She avoided him for the rest of the day, hoping that in her absence he would cool down and forgive her.

On Friday afternoon, Ellen worked late. Andrée left the lab at half past five. Time passed and the distant hum of a vacuum cleaner announced that Mary, the cleaner, had started her work. The house was quiet, and it occurred to Ellen that she and Mary might be the only ones still there.

Her work absorbed her, and by the time she had written up her notes and put away her equipment, the vacuum cleaner was long silent and the windowpanes enclosed squares of inky black sky. She turned off the light and shut the door of the lab behind her, then went to the box room to get her coat. She was doing up her buttons when the overhead light went out, plunging the box room into blackness. She fumbled for the switch and flicked it on and off: nothing. Picking up her briefcase and handbag, she felt for the doorknob, then stumbled out into the corridor.

After a few moments, her eyes accustomed themselves to the darkness, and she saw, above the condensation on a windowpane, speckles of stars. She knew that the stairs down to the first floor led off the corridor ahead, and with the flat of her hand against the wall for guidance began to move cautiously towards them. Her shin struck something hard and cold and she cried out. Stooping, her fingers padded first over sand and then touched the metal edge of the fire bucket, the same fire bucket in which she had found Dr Redmond's pen. She recalled the layout of the corridor, the fire bucket only a few feet from the topmost stair. Her right hand scooped shapes in the darkness until she found the round wooden ball of the finial at the top of the banister.

She was slowly descending the stairs when she heard

39

the sound. A pitter-pattering, scampering sound, like a child's footsteps. She froze. She could not tell where it was coming from. *A little boy died in the house, fell down the stairs,* Martin had told her. *You're supposed to be able to hear his footsteps at night, running up and down the corridors.*

The pitter-pattering was from above her – or no, perhaps it came from below. Or perhaps it was coming up the stairs towards her. A cry escaped her throat, and then the beating of her heart enmeshed with the sound of footsteps, louder and heavier than that dreadful pattering.

A circle of light swung up the stairs to her. 'Who is it?' someone called out. 'Who's there?'

She recognized Alec Hunter's voice. 'It's me!' she cried. 'Ellen Kingsley!'

'Are you all right?'

The torchlight swept up to her face and she put up a hand to her eyes. 'I'm fine.'

'You look as if you've had a fright.'

'I banged my leg against the fire bucket, that's all. And I thought I heard . . .'

'What?'

'There was a sound . . . Martin told me there were ghosts in the hall and I thought . . .' She broke off, feeling very foolish.

'Martin talks a lot of nonsense,' Alec said shortly. 'You shouldn't listen to him. Are you on your way home? Come, take my hand and we'll find our way out together.'

His touch reassured; slowly, they made their way

downstairs. 'I expect what I heard was Mr Gosse's dog,' she said. 'How idiotic of me to get into such a panic.'

'The mind can play tricks, especially at night.'

'So long as you don't tell the others.'

'I'm not one for tittle-tattle, Miss Kingsley. This place seethes with gossip. We work too closely together and we're too cut off from the world.'

His sudden hostility took her by surprise. She had meant it as a joke. Then she remembered Martin, in the pub, gleefully telling her of Alec Hunter's affair with Andrée Fournier, and thought she understood why he might dislike gossip.

'I'm sorry,' she said. 'I didn't mean to imply anything. How sensible of you, to have a torch.'

'I was in the basement. The lights often go out down there so I always keep a torch handy. It'll be the generator. Gosse will fix it.'

They followed the sweep of the torchlight through the house, down the stairs to the hallway. Alec said, 'I'll see you to the bike shed.'

'There's no need,' she began, but he had already opened the front door and was heading down the steps.

Her shin hurt where she had hit it on the fire bucket. She noticed that the air was growing colder. They crossed the courtyard to the path that led round by the side of the house. The gravel crunched beneath their feet and the bobbing light of the torch showed now and then the dim shapes of the outhouses and the dripping rows of winter vegetables in

41

the kitchen gardens. Alec said, 'How are you settling into Gildersleve Hall?' and she answered, 'Very well, I'm enjoying it very much,' and all the while, as they conversed, she was aware of his presence and the compulsion to look, to touch, to prolong this moment.

As they reached the bike shed, she glimpsed out of the corner of her eye a tremulous, flickering blaze in the windows of Gildersleve Hall as the lights went back on, illuminating Alec Hunter's features. And the pang of yearning she felt was sharp and foreign to her, because she was unused to longing for what she could not have.

Dr Pharoah's house was large and imposing, late Victorian or Edwardian, and surrounded by a garden and yew hedge. By the time Ellen arrived there at midday on Sunday, several cars were already parked in the driveway.

That morning, she felt ruffled. Ruffled by the headwind which had buffeted her, cycling from Copfield, ruffled by the memories which burned in her like an intermittent fever: the touch of Alec Hunter's hand and the fragmentary glimpses of him that Friday's blackout had allowed – a profile, the flash of a dark blue, almond-shaped eye.

She propped her bicycle against the wall of Dr Pharoah's house. The door to the porch was open and the black and white tiles inside it were strewn with wellington boots and a girl's coat, lavender wool with a purple velvet collar. She rang the bell. A few moments later a middle-aged woman opened the door.

Ellen introduced herself. Her coat and beret were taken and she was shown through to the drawing room. She made a quick mental adjustment. Sunday lunch at the Pharoahs' was no intimate family get-together: there must have been twenty people in the room. The walls and curtains were papered pale primrose and cream, and French windows looked out to a terrace on which stood stone urns, garlanded with ivy. Paintings hung on the walls, some abstract and bright, others darkened by age. Arrangements of autumn leaves and berries cascaded out of vases on the mantelpiece and tables.

Alison Pharoah was in her mid-thirties, slim and of medium height. Her flaxen hair was cut short, waving round her slightly snub nose, round eyes and small, full mouth. She was wearing a white pleated skirt and a white angora sweater, set off with a row of pearls. One of her hands was playing with the pearls. Ellen noticed that her nails were very short, and that the skin around them was ragged and torn, in contrast with the rest of her immaculate appearance.

Mrs Pharoah asked, 'Have you travelled far, Miss Kingsley?'

'Only a couple of miles. I live in Copfield.'

'Did you drive?'

'No, I cycled.'

'Cycled!' Mrs Pharoah's eyebrows raised. 'In this weather?'

'I don't mind, I'm used to it. I cycle to work each day.'

Throughout their brief conversation, Mrs Pharoah's eyes had remained cold. 'Gin and tonic all right?' she said. 'Heather will get you one. Let me introduce you to the

Dorringtons. Margaret Dorrington is a keen sportswoman. I'm sure you'll have a great deal in common.'

Ellen was talking to the Dorringtons – he was a GP, she played tennis at a club in Cambridge – when Dr Pharoah joined them. He greeted her.

'Thank you for inviting me, Dr Pharoah,' she said.

'Marcus.' He smiled. 'You must call me Marcus.'

A tall, grey-haired man, catching sight of Pharoah, said, 'Marcus, where have you been hiding? We want to hear about Chinon.'

'Damned rainy,' said Pharoah. 'I've been showing Devlin my latest acquisitions in the cellar.' He turned back to the Dorringtons. 'Jimmy, Margot, so glad you could make it. Do you know Miss Kingsley?'

'We've been talking about tennis,' said Mrs Dorrington.

'Are you a tennis player, Ellen?' asked Dr Pharoah.

'Only a very amateur one.'

'You must come and play on our court in the summer. It doesn't get enough use. I haven't time and Alison isn't keen.'

If Mrs Pharoah's pale iciness chilled, Dr Pharoah's warmth melted. Ellen murmured thanks.

Margaret Dorrington said, 'I thought Rowena was shaping up to be a nice little player.'

Pharoah smiled. 'I believe she is.'

'You should get her a coach. Makes all the difference at her age.'

Another man joined them. His arched black eyebrows

and the deep channels to either side of his mouth gave him a saturnine look.

'The Côtes Hermitage with the lamb, I should say.'

'Not the claret?'

'No, too young. The Côtes.' The dark, mocking gaze took in Ellen. 'Well, hello there. Who's this, Marc?'

'This is Ellen Kingsley. She works at the hall. She's a very clever and promising young lady and we're fortunate to have her with us. Ellen, meet my brother, Devlin.'

They shook hands. 'One of Marcus's brainboxes, then,' said Devlin Pharoah.

'Not really.' Ellen could see a family similarity, though in Devlin the Pharoah handsomeness had a rakish cast. 'Dr Pharoah was being kind. Most of my colleagues at Gildersleve Hall are far more erudite than I am.'

'Not so pretty, I imagine. I visited the place once and some of the female scientists were frightful frumps.'

'Are you a scientist yourself, Mr Pharoah?'

He laughed. 'I'm not nearly noble enough for that. Too much like hard work. I'm an antique dealer. I have a few shops in London to keep me busy.'

A voice called out, 'Daddy! Daddy!' A girl of twelve or so had run into the room. She ducked through the crowd to Marcus Pharoah's side.

'Hello, darling.' Pharoah put his arm round his daughter's shoulders.

Rowena Pharoah was a strikingly beautiful child, tall and slim, with her father's strong colouring. She was wearing

45

a turquoise wool dress with an embroidered belt, and her dark brown hair was in plaits.

'Daddy,' she said. 'I hate Rufus. He's so mean.'

'What's he done this time, Ro?' asked Devlin Pharoah.

'He's taken my wellies and won't give them back.' Rowena's voice took on a whining tone. 'He says he's going to throw them in the pond.'

'Christ, that boy,' muttered Devlin. He marched out of the room.

'Say hello to Miss Kingsley, Rowena,' said Dr Pharoah.

'Hello,' muttered Rowena. 'Daddy?'

'Yes, darling?'

'Can me and Rufus have lunch in the summer house?'

'Rufus and I,' corrected Pharoah. 'No, not this time, it's too cold.'

'*Daddy*. I'll wear my coat.'

'No, darling, I want you to eat your lunch with us. Besides, I thought you hated Rufus.'

'He's a very silly boy,' Rowena said condescendingly.

'Have you helped Heather with the table?'

'No.' A black patent sandal was scuffed along the carpet.

'Run along then, sweetheart.'

'Daddy, I don't *want* to.'

Pharoah coaxed, 'But you like choosing the glasses.'

'Do it with me, *please*, Daddy.'

Pharoah smiled at his daughter fondly. 'Would you excuse me, Ellen?'

He and Rowena left the room. The Dorringtons had

moved on to talk to someone else. Through the French windows, Ellen could see Devlin Pharoah remonstrating with a wild-looking, dark-haired boy of around Rowena's age. The wind brushed the plumes of the pampas grass and Ellen ran her conversation with Alec Hunter through her head again, testing it, tasting it, as she had done countless times since Friday evening, and felt a heady delight.

A sound from behind her made her look round. The housekeeper was gathering glasses on to a tray. Ellen made her way to the dining room.

Apart from Rowena and Rufus and a scattering of children, Ellen was the youngest person at the table. No one else from Gildersleve Hall had been invited. The talk over lunch was of plays seen and concerts attended, of holidays in Cornwall or Scotland or undiscovered parts of France.

'The Pattersons' friends, do you remember them from New Year?'

'When there's a storm, the spray hits the windows.'

'Charlie and John go fishing and we don't see them from dawn to dusk.'

'The mountains are still full of bandits. We thought our throats would be cut before we reached Turin.'

'Have you come far, Miss Kingsley? And how do you know the Pharoahs?'

Ellen explained, briefly, to the solicitor sitting beside her, about X-ray crystallography, and then, when she judged that he had had enough, listened to him talk about yachting. She saw how Mrs Pharoah ensured that the serving of the

47

meal went off smoothly and unobtrusively, how she made sure her guests had everything they wanted, nodding to the housekeeper to let her know when to clear a course. No wine glass was left empty and every guest was drawn into the conversation.

She saw how Devlin Pharoah talked and smiled, though now and then his gaze drifted away. Was it boredom she saw in those black eyes, or contempt? The two cousins, Rowena and Rufus, sat side by side, Rowena whispering to her cousin, covering her mouth with her hand. 'Not at the table, Rowy, it's impolite,' murmured Alison Pharoah, but when she looked away the whispering started again. When fruit was served at the end of the meal, Rufus flicked orange pips with finger and thumb, pinging them off wine glasses, until his father said angrily, 'That's enough, Rufe.'

Lunch ended with a haze of cigarette smoke and a shuffling of chairs. Groups of guests dispersed through the house. Women talked in low voices of errant children and obstetric disasters, and some of the men sprawled in armchairs, making jokes, roaring with laughter. The Dorringtons were sitting in silence, not part of any group. They were makeweights, Ellen suspected, like herself.

She went to find a bathroom. Copies of Punch on a small wicker table and a bottle of Blue Grass hand lotion. She checked her face in the mirror and ran a comb through her hair; she scooped it up so that it surrounded her features like Alison Pharoah's, then let it fall to her shoulders again.

She reached down and rubbed the bruise on her leg, and felt the raised ridge left by the metal edge of the fire bucket.

On the way back to the drawing room, she looked through an open door and saw Dr Pharoah. He beckoned to her. 'Come and have a look at this, Ellen.'

She went inside the room. He pointed at a photograph. 'This was taken during the war,' he said. 'You can see the fences and barbed wire.'

In the picture, Gildersleve Hall looked muted and dingy and the wide sweep of trees that surrounded it blocked the horizon. The ivy that now grew only over the tower spread like an infection over the entire house.

Pharoah said, 'We worked twelve-hour days back then. Exhausting, but I never minded. We were young, I suppose. See this, Ellen.' He indicated another photo. 'I took this the day I knew the hall was mine. It had been empty for a year and was in a pretty rough state, but our first scientists moved in three months later. I did a lot of the work myself.' He laughed. 'I remember climbing over the roof to sort out some slates. If I'd slipped, that would have been the end of Gildersleve Hall.'

There was a footfall and Devlin Pharoah came into the room. 'Thought you might want to dig out those papers for me, Marc. Not interrupting anything, am I?'

His words had an implication that Ellen disliked. She murmured her excuses and slipped out of the door. Along the corridor, china and glasses and the stained cloth still lay on the dining table. Only Rowena and Rufus remained

49

in the room, sitting side by side on the deep windowsill, whispering. Ellen thought Rufus looked dissolute, like his father. Silly of her – he was only a child. Rufus grabbed the girl's plaits, one in each hand, and gave them a hard tug. 'Ow, stop it, Rufe,' moaned Rowena, but Rufus did it again, jerking her towards him so that their faces were only an inch apart, and this time Rowena let out shrill laughter.

'Do you know where your mother is, Rowena?' said Ellen, and Rufus let go of the plaits.

Rowena shrugged. 'Haven't an earthly. Sorry.'

At the end of a corridor Ellen discovered a small pink and green room. Though it was no doubt charming in summer, with its white-painted chairs and bookcases of paperbacks and boardgames, the room seemed cold and unwelcoming in late October. Ellen saw a movement in the wood and glass structure that led off from the glazed side door. On the chest-height benches were orchids in pots. Their petals were pink and green and yellow, spotted and speckled, contorted and velvety, some protruding like tongues.

Alison Pharoah was in there, smoking a cigarette as she looked out of a window. Ellen was about to offer to help with the clearing up when she saw that Mrs Pharoah was crying. Her tears were silent, she hardly seemed to notice them, and while she cried she tore at her nails and the flesh around them with her teeth. A bead of blood glimmered on her finger like a ruby.

Quietly, Ellen left the room. All those people in the house, she thought, all those Jimmys and Devs and Rufes, and there was Alison Pharoah, crying alone in her conservatory. Glancing at her watch, she saw that it was past three o'clock.

Her earlier elation had vanished, replaced by staleness. The glamour of the Pharoahs' lives seemed to mask a darker undertow, and now she also saw her encounter with Alec on Friday night through more rational eyes, a conversation with a colleague, of slight significance. She longed to leave, to return to the quiet of her room at Mrs Bryant's bungalow. After thanking Marcus Pharoah for his hospitality, she fetched her coat and hat and cycled home.

Chapter Two

November: rooks jabbed their bills at the iron clods of earth and frost greyed the fields. Icy winds leaked through the gaps round the doors and windows of Gildersleve Hall. Making up salt solutions in which to float haemoglobin crystals, Ellen's hands were clumsy with cold. She noted down the size and shape of the crystals, their colouration and peculiarities and imperfections. As she adjusted the microscope, patterns shifted beneath the lens.

Alec Hunter was at the bike shed when she went there at the end of the day. Ellen said, 'Cold, isn't it?'

He looked around as if he hadn't noticed the ice and the frost and said politely, 'Yes, very.'

She wondered whether he had been waiting for her.

They walked their bicycles side by side down the path. She half-expected him to cycle off as soon as they reached the courtyard – a wave of the hand, a fast pedalling away as Alec Hunter went off to do whatever Alec Hunter did on an evening – but instead he walked on, scarcely attempting to respond to her efforts at small talk.

The cypresses beside the drive walled them off from the hall. Alec said, 'I heard Pharoah invited you to Sunday lunch.'

'Yes.' Now, there was a surprise: of all the things she might have thought – hoped, if she was honest with herself – he might be working himself up to say, that had not been one of them. She said, 'It was very pleasant.'

'Good.'

Weighted silences had never been to her taste, so she plodded on. 'Have you been to his house?'

'Me? No. Not Pharoah's sort.'

A strange remark. Mustn't they all be Pharoah's sort, those he had chosen to work at Gildersleve Hall?

They reached the end of the drive. The lamplight cast black pools of shadow on Alec's face. He said, 'I wanted to say – be careful, Ellen.'

'Careful? Of what?' Tension made her touchy. 'I didn't spill my wine down my front or eat off my knife, if that's what you mean.'

'No, of course not.' His scowl deepened. 'What do you think of Pharoah?'

'He's an extraordinary man. He's achieved so much.'

'You've had predecessors, you know. Some of them weren't quite good enough, and others . . . well, let's just say they didn't fit in.'

53

'I know I've a lot to prove. I work hard.'

He ran a hand through his hair. He wasn't wearing gloves or a hat: she wondered whether he did it for effect – tough, Scottish, in tune with the elements.

'Pharoah takes a liking to people sometimes,' he said. 'And that's all very nice if it's you he's taken a liking to, and while he's still keen on you, but if you disappoint for some reason, well.'

She felt a wash of disillusionment. *So that's what you think of me, Alec Hunter. You think I'm not good enough at my job.* She said coldly, 'I don't intend to disappoint.'

'Sometimes it can happen, even when you do your best. Pharoah can blow hot and cold. It might be wise to keep a wee bit of distance.'

'I hardly think Marcus Pharoah and I are likely to be close friends.' And what business was it of his anyway? 'We don't inhabit the same world.'

'Pharoah has his pets and it doesn't do to say no to him.'

Now she was angry. 'I've no intention of being anyone's pet.'

A flicker of annoyance crossed his face. 'I'm only trying to help you, Ellen.'

'I don't need anyone's help. I'll manage on my own. I always have.' Her voice was as crisp and cold as the ice that fringed the leaves of the cypresses.

They had reached the gates. She climbed on to her bicycle, bid him a curt goodbye, and cycled away.

*   *   *

54

On Sunday afternoon, Ellen went out for a long walk. The branches of the trees stood out dark and jagged against a bleached background as she tramped round the edges of the fields. The water in the gullies and ditches had frozen and was pierced by spikes of cow parsley; when she broke off a frond it gave a brittle snap, powdering the ice with fragments of stem. She thought, how dare he? How dare he tell me how to do my job, or how to behave towards my employer? It was not as if he himself was without fault. Alec Hunter, presumably, must himself be responsible for a great deal of Andrée's ill humour.

An hour of walking and she passed Gildersleve Hall, heading through the copse behind the house. The blinds were down and nothing moved in the garden. The house seemed to have retreated in on itself, as secretive as the very first time she had seen it, cycling from Copfield.

A wooden fingerpost directed her to Peddar's Wood. Circling round bare fields she reached a mass of trees surrounded by a low ridge of earth. A footpath led beneath maples, ashes and hazel. She headed into the woodland, the soles of her boots crunching on frozen leaves. Stacks of cut logs, their bark glistening with frost, lay beside the path, and the ash trees were coppiced into extraordinary shapes, great, bulbous globes that grew close to the soil. From the boles, thick branches reached up to the sky, and from the smaller, pale, hollow trunks, whiskery shoots protruded, as thin as a whip.

In the heartland of the wood, Ellen stood motionless,

her fingers aching with cold. The trees were timeless, dislocating her from the present, and she felt herself surrounded by such silence and stillness that when the crack of a branch told her she was not the only living creature in the wood, she jumped.

Catching sight of a man some distance ahead of her, at a place where the footpaths formed a crossroads, she recognized Dr Redmond. He was loading fallen twigs and branches into a wheelbarrow.

She called out to him and he looked up. She said, as she drew level with him, 'Are you collecting firewood?'

'Kindling.' The front of his duffel coat was sprinkled with leaf mould and flakes of bark. 'I leave the bigger pieces. Insects live in them and fungi grows on the rotten wood.'

'It's a beautiful place.'

'The wood was neglected when I first came here. All the trees needed coppicing. Farmers don't care about woodland any more, it doesn't make them any money. When the trees grow too tall they shut out the sunlight and then there are no spring flowers. I try to cut them back every four or five years. I've kept a record of every species I've found here since I came to live at the cottage. The first spring, there were only a dozen oxlips. Last year, there were so many I was able to do merely an approximate tally.'

Dr Redmond began to wheel the barrow along another footpath, at right angles to the one Ellen had taken from the fields. Walking beside him, she said, 'Your cottage is near here, isn't it?'

'By the farm track.'

'How long have you lived there?'

'Ten years. There was a shortage of lodgings in the war. You wouldn't have had a house like that to yourself back then. The three of us shared it, Kaminski, Pharoah and me.'

They came out of the woodland on to a broad track. The barrow rattled along the solid, rutted ground. A short distance along stood a small, brick-built house. Ellen found it hard to imagine: the three men, young then, and so unalike in character and experience. Pharoah, brilliant and ambitious, Kaminski, exiled and damaged, and Redmond – but it was impossible to picture Dr Redmond as a young man. Had they eaten together after a long day at work? Had they smoked cigarettes and drunk beer and laughed and planned their futures?

They reached the cottage. Opening the front door, Dr Redmond took out a battered coal scuttle and put it on the porch. He began to fill it with kindling.

She said curiously, 'You've known Dr Pharoah for a long time, haven't you, Dr Redmond?'

'Since before the war. After he came back from America, after his wife died. We worked together.'

She was going to make some comment – old friends, the pleasures of scientific collaboration – when his face contorted and he said savagely, 'He's changed. He was a better man, then. Marcus Pharoah is a liar and a plagiarist, but he won't get away with it. The rest of that lot might let him, but I won't!'

Then he rolled the wheelbarrow round the side of the house, leaving Ellen standing by the doorstep.

Wednesday evening: Ellen was sitting in the bar of the University Arms Hotel in Cambridge and Dr Pharoah was giving their order to the waiter. 'A lemonade, please,' Ellen said, and Dr Pharoah said, 'I think you need a gin in that, after that meeting. A gin and lemon, please, waiter, and a Johnnie Walker, water, no ice.' And, turning to her with a smile, 'Rather a marathon. These things sometimes seem to go on for ever. I hope you weren't too bored.'

'Not at all, Dr Pharoah.' Then, 'Sorry. Marcus.'

There had been three of them that afternoon at the meeting at the Cavendish: Ellen, flattered and excited to be asked along, Dr Pharoah and Dr Farmborough. As they had left the laboratory at half past six, Dr Farmborough had peeled off into the night. 'Have to see a man about a dog.'

The other tables in the bar were occupied by men in suits, flicking through newspapers or importantly checking their wristwatches. Ellen thought, I'm in a smart hotel in Cambridge, having a drink with Marcus Pharoah, the director of Gildersleve Hall. Outside, the city glittered like glass, trapped in the frost. A mist blurred the outlines of the buildings, as if they existed underwater.

'I'm afraid such meetings are part and parcel of scientific life,' Dr Pharoah was saying. 'You'll find it a useful asset, the ability to look interested when you've heard the same argument half a dozen times before.' Their drinks arrived and he touched the rim of his glass against hers. 'To your long and successful career, Ellen.'

'Thank you.'

'Tell me about yourself. Have you family?'

'Parents and a younger brother.'

His dark, hooded eyes studied her, serious, interested. Being the object of Marcus Pharoah's undivided attention made you feel significant, in a way you had not felt before. It made you feel worth listening to. But it was also a little unsettling.

'Would you like Rowena to be a scientist, Marcus?'

He smiled. 'I should love her to be one, especially if she managed to do so while being as charming and attractive as you and Mademoiselle Fournier. But she isn't the least bit interested in science, I'm afraid, and at the moment has her mind set on doing something with her art.'

'How marvellous.'

'Yes, I think so. She'll go to college when the time comes – unless, that is, some young man snaps her up before then.'

A woman in a pearl-grey evening coat came into the bar; one of the businessmen rose and kissed her cheek.

Ellen said, 'You have such a beautiful home. And Alison's so lovely and gracious. It must make such a difference, being able to rely on someone else for all the – oh, I don't know . . .'

'The background work? The running of the house, the

59

entertaining, the bringing up of children? Yes, it does make a difference. Although Alison hasn't been well.'

Alison Pharoah, weeping among her orchids. *Oh*, she thought. 'I'm sorry. I didn't realize.'

'I haven't told many people. Such things are better kept private. The hall has a reputation for gossip. I'm sure you'll keep it to yourself, Ellen.'

'I won't mention it to anyone.'

'Thank you, I knew you'd understand. Family life . . . You haven't been tempted, then?'

She was confused. 'By what?'

'By marriage.'

'No, not at all.'

He was sitting relaxed in his chair, his amused gaze focused on her. 'I'd hate to think we might lose you to domesticity,' he said.

'There's not much chance of that. Maybe one day, in the future. Most women marry eventually, don't they?'

The corners of his mouth curled. 'You sound as though you have it all worked out.'

She wondered whether he was laughing at her. Whether he thought her temporary, not a stayer. 'Women have to plan better than men because we have children,' she said. 'A man can be a little more free and easy. I can't afford that.'

'I do understand. I lost several years of my career to the war effort.' Without asking her, Pharoah signalled to the waiter for two more drinks. 'What first attracted you to science, Ellen?'

'I wanted to be part of making the future.' Enthused, she sat forward, her elbows on the arms of her chair. 'Such wonderful things are happening, aren't they? Think of the diseases we can cure now, tuberculosis, pneumonia, diphtheria – all those old killers. I want to be a part of everything, not just watching it happen from the sidelines.'

'You're very passionate, Ellen.'

Abruptly, she felt deflated. Men said that sort of thing to women: she had talked too much, had allowed her emotions to show.

Pharoah seemed to sense her discomfiture because he reached out and put a hand on her arm. 'It's all right, Ellen, passion's a quality I admire in a scientist. You could have a very promising future at Gildersleve, you know that, don't you? We're all ambitious, of course, and some will be successful and some won't. I always tell my new recruits that to succeed, you have to get everything right. Being clever isn't enough.'

Was that a warning? His hand still lay lightly on her forearm, the palm strong and square, the fingers long, well-shaped, even sensual. It was a kind, consoling gesture, she told herself, and she had no reason to feel discomforted, nor oddly disorientated, as if the fog in the streets had entered the room and the usual yardstick by which she measured events had slipped away. But voices echoed, blurred by the gin she had drunk too hastily to keep up with him. Alec Hunter's: *Pharoah has his pets.* Dr Redmond's: *Marcus Pharoah is a liar and a plagiarist.*

The waiter arrived with the drinks. Ellen thanked him and Marcus Pharoah's hand fell away. Half a dozen people came into the hotel, the women unknotting silk scarves and laughing, the men talking loudly of cars, sparking up cigarettes.

She broke the silence. 'What attracted you to science, Marcus?'

'Oh, as you say, the desire to be part of progress, to be at the forefront of new ideas.' He laughed. 'When I was young, I ran around like a wind-up toy that's been set off, expounding my latest ideas to all and sundry. Rather like Martin. But then . . .' He broke off, frowning, and his voice dropped. 'I had such ambition then, such vision,' he muttered.

The alteration in Marcus Pharoah was as if someone had drawn a curtain, shutting out the light. You would have thought, if you had glimpsed him sitting alone in a bar: another morose middle-aged man, looking for comfort in the bottom of a glass.

'When we're young, we think that if we do this and that, then we'll feel content.' He picked up his glass, swirled the contents. 'Even a little bit pleased with ourselves. We don't realize that the fear of failure never quite goes away.'

She was astonished. 'But you must feel so proud of what you've achieved at Gildersleve Hall.'

He gave a light laugh. 'Yes, naturally.'

Ellen glanced at her watch. 'I should catch my bus. Thank you for the drinks, Marcus.'

'There's no need to rush off.' He, too, looked at his watch. 'I have to stay on in town for an appointment later this evening. Why don't we go on to dinner somewhere?'

She was drawn by his voice, by its rich, coaxing quality, and by the compelling gaze of his eyes. When he looked at you like that, when he spoke to you like that, you wanted to please him. You'd do anything for him, almost anything.

And yet, in the back of her mind, the crystal of doubt hardened and glittered. 'I can't, I'm afraid,' she said with a smile. 'My landlady cooks supper for seven. I can't just not turn up, it wouldn't be fair.'

'Telephone her, Ellen.'

'She hasn't a phone, I'm afraid.'

'Then I'm sure she'll understand.' She read a challenge in his eyes.

'No, I'm sorry, I really must get back. If I hurry, there's a bus.' She rose, almost knocking over her glass in her hurry, holding out her hand.

Pharoah, too, stood up. 'It's been most interesting.'

Hurrying along St Andrew's Street, Ellen noticed that though the mist lingered, a few flakes of snow had begun to drift through the air. Her breath made vapour clouds as she ran through their conversation in her head. Had it been an act of friendship, that invitation for a drink, or had it been some sort of unofficial checking-up, a gentle hint that if she wanted to remain at Gildersleve Hall then she must improve, raise her game?

Or had it been been something more than that? It seemed

to her that they had moved too easily to the personal, the intimate. *Alison hasn't been well for some time.* There had been the implication, she thought, in Marcus Pharoah's words, that Alison was suffering from an illness of the mind. Why had he told her that? Had he simply needed to confide in someone? Was power and position so isolating that sometimes, worn down with obligations and with the added burden of a sick wife, you found yourself opening your heart to the lowest of the low? She remembered the weight of his hand on hers, the pressure of his fingertips.

Her bus was pulling away from its stop. She ran across the road and climbed on to the platform. The interior smelled of metal and rubber and cigarette smoke. You fool, Ellen, she thought as she found a seat, running away like a prim schoolgirl when you could have been dining with Marcus Pharoah. When you think of all he could offer you.

But that was the thing. What, exactly, had been on offer? Dinner at a restaurant, or something more? Somewhere along the line, the conversation had taken an uncomfortable turn. Was that what Alec had been warning her against, during their conversation the other day? But why should Alec Hunter be concerned that Dr Pharoah was showing an interest in Ellen Kingsley? Was Alec a confidant of Dr Pharoah's? She did not think so. It was Pharoah with whom Alec argued at the seminars, Pharoah's contributions he seemed to take most pleasure in picking apart.

There was so much she did not understand. Undercurrents seethed at Gildersleve Hall, factionalism, old enmities and rivalries, and it occurred to her, as she watched from the window the snowflakes whirling in the yellow light of the street lamps, that she felt more of an outsider now than she had on her very first day at the hall.

By Monday morning, a light dusting of snow had settled on the roof of the hall and the crenellations of the tower. Cycling along the path, Ellen heard the thud, thud, of Gosse's axe, as he chopped up wood.

Her eye was caught by a flash of red in the copse. She saw that Alec Hunter and Andrée Fournier were standing beneath the trees, talking. Andrée was wearing her grey coat and scarlet scarf, and her hands waved gestures as her mouth opened and closed. Ellen wondered whether she was crying. Alec's hand rested on Andrée's sleeve: Ellen felt a little stab to her heart.

Inside the hall, cold air tumbled down the chimneys, lurking like a poltergeist in the corners of the rooms. Toby was off sick; half the staff seemed to have colds or flu. Andrée, red-eyed and white-faced, came into the box room while Ellen was taking off her coat. Her head was splitting, she felt ill, she said. She was going back home to bed.

Ellen spent the morning measuring the intensities of the dots on X-ray diffraction photographs and beginning the complex mathematical calculations that would help Dr Kaminski interpret them. There were frost flowers on the insides of the window and she broke off now and then to rub the circulation back into her fingers. With both Toby and Andrée away, the top floor of the hall was quiet, only the distant percussion of Dr Redmond's sneezes from the tower punctuating the silence.

That afternoon, she heard them arguing again, Dr Pharoah and Dr Redmond, in the tower. The rise and fall of their voices was ominous and angry, like the drumbeat of Roy Gosse's axe. She went outside and stood in the corridor. The door to the tower was ajar; she pushed it open further.

'Why can't you leave me alone?' Dr Redmond's voice.

'Leave you alone?' Dr Pharoah was speaking. 'What, and have you lurking up here, like some goddamned spider, spreading poison? Not any more.'

'I'll make sure everyone knows the truth about you! I'll tell them everything!' Redmond's words had soared in pitch. 'I could destroy you, you know! I've got proof and I'll use it, don't think I won't!'

Ellen slipped back into the lab, silently closing the door behind her. The air seemed to vibrate; when she sat down at the bench, she felt her heart thump hard as she looked down the microscope, and she had to blink to focus her gaze on the geometric shape of the crystal.

More snow fell that night. The following morning, she had to push the bike much of the way to work, pitting her strength against the clogged inches of snow. A stillness had settled over the countryside, nothing moved.

In the laboratory, she found herself listening for sounds from the tower. No sneezes today, no footsteps. After weeks of careful work, her crystals had clumped together in a disordered mass, no use to anyone. She put the lot down the sink and started again. She couldn't concentrate, her mind was all over the place, skittering about, refusing to latch on to any one thing.

At midday, she went into the tower. The door to Dr Redmond's lab was shut. She tapped on it and went inside. The lab was empty, and she thought how strange it was that you could sense, lacking any solid evidence, that a room had been empty all day.

She had intended to work late that evening but she was tired, and by six o'clock the numbers had begun to swim before her eyes. She put on her outdoor things, then went to the shed and put her briefcase and handbag in her bicycle basket. Then, taking only her purse and torch, she set off over the fields.

From Gildersleve Hall, the walk to Peddar's Wood was less than a mile. The cold bit into her fingers and toes and her torchlight split the snow crystals into jewelled colours. Several times she wondered whether to turn back. Dr Redmond had probably stayed at home for the day because he had fallen out with Dr Pharoah. Or his cold had worsened and he had spent the day in bed. He wouldn't welcome her, coming to see him.

Yet the unease that had haunted her all day remained, so she kept on walking. The torch lit her way, revealing the smooth layer of snow that covered the hedgerows and fields. Inside Peddar's Wood, the trees had kept the narrow path free from snow.

She came to the crossroads where she had met Dr Redmond loading his barrow with kindling and struck off down the wider path to the left, towards the single-track road. Reaching it, she saw that light issued from the cottage windows and felt relieved. He was all right, he had taken a day off because he was unwell, that was all, silly of her to worry. She noticed that there were no footprints in the fresh snow on the farm track.

She knocked on the door of the cottage. When there was no answer, she looked through a window. She saw that the room was disordered, books pulled from the shelves and thrown to the floor. She turned the handle on the front door; it was unlocked.

She went inside the house. The door led straight into the living room she had seen through the window. 'Dr Redmond?' she called out.

No answer. Her gaze slid round the room, taking in the two armchairs, their coverings shiny with age, a threadbare sofa and a heavy, old-fashioned table and chairs. There were ashes in the grate and some of the books that had fallen on to the frayed rug had crumpled pages and broken spines. A handful of photographs scattered the floor. She picked one up. It was a snapshot of a hazel tree, pollarded like those in the wood.

A narrow kitchen, furnished with a ceramic sink, calor gas cooker and cupboard, led off from the living room. Here, too, drawers were open and the contents scattered around. A saucepan on the hob contained something brown and unidentifiable, and there was a saucer with scraps of bread and fat on the sill, for feeding birds, presumably. A mug of tea stood on the table, covered with a pale brown scum. When she touched her hand to its side, the scum swayed, heavy, frozen.

As in the lab, the house felt empty. Dr Redmond might have gone away. He might have parents, a brother, a friend to visit. A door led off from the living room, to the stairs presumably, and it occurred to her that she should check the upper storey of the house. He might be ill, his cold might have turned to flu. He might be gasping through lungs like sponges for every fluid-soaked breath, no one to help him, no other house for miles.

She tried the handle of the door. It opened an inch, no further. Something was blocking it, preventing it from opening properly. She tried again, pushing with her shoulder against the door until she was able to reach her fingers into the aperture.

Her fingertips touched cloth. The cloth felt ridged, like corduroy. She thought of the shabby corduroy jacket Dr Redmond wore at the lab every day, and her heart thudded. Like thinking you had reached the bottom of the stairs when there was one more to go, jarring, shocking.

Ellen leaned her whole weight against the door, then wedged her foot into the gap. Shoulder first, she squeezed through the opening and almost fell over Dr Redmond's body.

He was lying at the foot of the stairs. His glasses were a

short distance from his outstretched hand, their lenses fractured into stars. She touched his fingers; they felt ice-cold. She was afraid to shine the torch on his face, but when she did so, she saw that his eyes remained a little open, as if he had wanted to have one last look at the world. And then they had dulled, the light and the life extinguished.

It felt wrong to leave him there alone. The thought clawed at her as she stumbled back along the farm track to the path through the woods, but she had no alternative. There was no telephone in the cottage, and no other houses in the vicinity.

Ellen began to run, looking back over her shoulder once or twice, as if something was chasing her. The branches of the trees struck her face, and when she swung her torch in front of her along the wide path, she saw that the snow was smooth and unblemished by her footprints. She had gone too far, had missed the crossroads in the middle of the wood and had overshot the turn-off. Her breath made fast puffs of vapour in the icy air and her torch shed only a small point of light in the dense darkness.

Think.

She retraced her footsteps until she found the path that would lead her through the trees, in the direction of Gildersleve Hall. As she jogged along it, her thoughts returned to the cheerless cottage, which had been scarcely warmer inside than outside, and which had contained little of any comfort. She thought of Dr Redmond himself and the peculiar manner that had been a part of him. All gone now, all that brilliance and strangeness extinguished.

Now she was out in the open fields. The moon illuminated the roof of Gildersleve Hall and the square summit of its tower. She ran along the edge of the field, the frozen ruts of the ploughed furrows hard against the soles of her feet, tripping and stumbling on the iron-hard mud until she reached the copse, then she swung the torch ahead of her as she threaded through the trees. As she took the gravel path that led to the side door of the hall, the adrenalin that had enabled her to run from the cottage began to fade, leaving her weak with shock and exhaustion.

Inside the building, she heard the steady hum of the hoover. Mary, the cleaner, looked up as she came into the corridor.

'You've cut your face, Miss Kingsley.'

Both Dr Pharoah's office and his secretary's were empty. Ellen sat down at the secretary's desk to use the phone. Her hands were trembling, her fingers nerveless. The operator put her through to the police station in Cambridge. As she was speaking, she looked up and saw Gosse standing in the doorway.

She finished the call and put the phone down. 'There's been an accident,' she said. 'It's Dr Redmond. I'm afraid he's dead. I've just been to his cottage. It looks as if he fell downstairs. I've phoned the police but someone needs to tell Dr Pharoah.'

Gosse pushed past her, snatching the phone receiver

71

from her. Ellen heard him dial a number as she left the room.

Something occurred to her, and she hurried up the stairs to the top floor of the house, then entered the tower and Dr Redmond's laboratory. There, she took the lab book from the bench, tucked it beneath her coat, and then, closing the doors behind her, left the tower. From below, she heard quick, heavy footsteps – Gosse's, she assumed.

Outside, in the bike shed, she took her briefcase out of her bicycle basket and put Dr Redmond's lab book inside it. Then she went back into the hall to wait for the police.

The call came through to the station shortly after half past seven: a sudden death at a cottage in the grounds of Gildersleve Hall, the science lab to the west of Cambridge. Detective Inspector John Riley took Sergeant Claybrooke with him and arranged for two more officers to meet them at the cottage. Claybrooke drove the Wolseley with conscientious, if slightly irritating slowness, along roads that were glazed with ice. There was little traffic on this cold December night and they were soon out in open country.

As they neared the turn-off that led to the cottage, the second police car rolled up behind them and they rattled down the frozen, rutted farm track in convoy. Riley had Claybrooke park some distance from the cottage and they walked the remainder of the way, torchlights sweeping across the path. Reaching the cottage, he saw footprints in the snow, heading away from the road towards the woods.

The front door was unlocked and Riley led the way inside. The body of Dr Redmond, who looked to be in his mid-forties, lay at the foot of the stairs. There was in all sudden deaths a pathos, a collision of mischance with an exposure of vulnerability, emphasized on this occasion by the cold, disorderly cottage. Riley automatically checked for a pulse but it was obvious to him that the man had been dead for some time.

He said over his shoulder, 'Is Dr Bell on his way?'

'Should be here any minute, sir,' Claybrooke replied.

Riley and Claybrooke remained at the cottage until the doctor arrived. Shortly afterwards they left for Gildersleve Hall. Driving along icy roads ranked by trees, Riley's mind drifted to his wife, Pearl. A week ago, they had moved house to London, after Pearl had tired of Cambridgeshire. Riley was working out his notice before returning in two weeks' time to the Metropolitan Police. How were they managing, Pearl and Annie, in the new house? Did the new home still amuse and enchant, or had disappointment already set in? Though Pearl always longed for change, it invariably disturbed her.

Sergeant Claybrooke swung the car through gates and along a gravel drive, and Riley saw Gildersleve Hall for the first time. As they parked, the front door opened and a short, burly man in a camouflage jacket came down the steps towards them. Riley greeted him and showed his warrant card.

The man in the camouflage jacket said, 'Dr Pharoah isn't here yet.'

Riley nodded. 'No matter. We'll speak to him when he arrives. Who are you?'

'Roy Gosse.' Gosse didn't offer his hand or any explanation of his role at Gildersleve. 'He was at some do,' he said. 'He's on his way.'

'Let me know when he gets here. I'd like to speak to Miss Kingsley now.'

They followed Gosse into the house. A wide, curving staircase led up from a hallway tiled in black and white marble. On the first floor, Gosse flung open a door to a small room, muttered something, then stalked off.

A young woman was sitting at a chair by a desk. She was huddled in her coat, her hands tucked beneath her arms as if she was trying to warm them. She looked up as they came into the room.

Riley estimated her to be in her early twenties. Her dark red hair was caught back with a clip and her eyes were grey. Her face was oval, her mouth full, her skin pale. Even with the long, thin cut across her cheek, which she dabbed at now and then with a folded handkerchief, she was strikingly attractive. Riley noted her apparent composure and the cup of tea in front of her, which she didn't look to have touched.

He said, 'Miss Kingsley?'

She rose, gave a shadow of a smile. 'Yes, I'm Ellen Kingsley.'

'I'm Inspector Riley and this is Sergeant Claybrooke.' They shook hands. 'Do sit down, Miss Kingsley. Would you like me to find someone to see to that cut?'

'No, thank you. It's nothing, just a scratch.'

'This must have been very unpleasant for you so I'll try not to keep you too long. Do you work at Gildersleve Hall?'

'Yes, I'm a research assistant.'

'Dr Redmond worked at the hall as well, didn't he?'

'Yes.' She put a hand towards the cup of tea, seemed to think better of it, and withdrew it. 'He was very senior to me.'

'Was he a friend of yours?'

'Not a friend.' Though Miss Kingsley looked shocked, her voice was firm. 'Dr Redmond didn't really have friends. I should say we were acquaintances.'

'And it was you who found the body?'

'Yes. I went to his cottage after work. I was worried about him.'

'Why was that?'

'He hadn't been into work and I thought he might be ill. He'd had a bad cold, you see. Colds and flu are going round the lab just now.'

'So you decided to go to his cottage. How did you get there?'

'I walked. There's a footpath through the woods.'

'How did you get inside?'

'The front door was unlocked.'

'Do you know if that was usual?'

'I'd only been there once before and it wasn't locked then. The cottage is miles from anywhere, so I don't expect he usually locks . . .'

Her words trailed off. Riley had noticed this many times before, that sense of shock people felt at the realization that they were speaking of someone in the wrong tense.

He prompted, 'So you went indoors.'

'Yes.' She recovered her composure. 'I had a look round and then I thought I'd better check upstairs, in case he was ill in bed. But I couldn't open the door to the stairs. He'd fallen in front of it, you see. When I saw him I knew he was dead.'

From outside, Riley heard the sound of a car engine, followed by a door opening and closing.

Miss Kingsley said, 'I think the cottage had been searched.'

'Searched?' The same thought had occurred to him.

'The place was a mess.' Her grey eyes held his, wide and troubled. 'There were things all over the living room floor. Dr Redmond wouldn't have left it like that.'

Voices from below: *Mildmay, damned unfortunate business, this.*

Superintendent Mildmay: *Pharoah, good to see you. I'm only sorry it should be in such tragic circumstances.* Then footsteps on the stairs.

Sergeant Claybrooke opened the door. Superintendent Mildmay – fiftyish, small, pale eyes, pink scalp dusted with thinning sandy hair – was standing on the landing. Beside him was a tall, dark man: Dr Marcus Pharoah, the head of Gildersleve Hall.

Superintendent Mildmay said, 'I'll take over now, thank you, Riley. You can get back to the cottage. Miss Kingsley, nasty shock for you. You may go home now.' The pale eyes drifted back to Riley. 'Inspector, do get a move on. Dr Pharoah hasn't got all day.'

Riley left the room.

Ellen heard the door to Dr Pharoah's office close. Through the adjoining wall, there was the murmur of voices. She looked down at the cup of tea she couldn't face drinking, which reminded her of the frozen mug of tea in Dr Redmond's house. She felt sick and dazed, and when she stood up, her legs shook.

She left the room and went downstairs. A voice said, 'Ellen.' Turning, she saw Alec Hunter.

'Someone told me what's happened,' he said. 'I was working downstairs. Poor Redmond. It's bloody awful. Hard to take in.'

She closed her eyes, shaking her head. She heard him say, 'You poor girl. Here, have some of this. It'll do you good.'

Alec took a flask out of his jacket pocket and handed it to her. Ellen swallowed a couple of mouthfuls of Scotch. It was smooth and fiery and tasted of the sea.

'Thank you,' she murmured.

'Where are you heading?'

'Back to my lodgings.'

'You live in Copfield, don't you? I'll see you home. Let me get my coat. Wait there.'

It was a relief to be told what to do; she sank into a chair and waited for him. A couple of minutes later he returned, buttoning his coat.

He opened the door for her and they went outside to collect her bike. Alec pushed her bicycle along the drive. Her briefcase was in the bicycle basket. She thought of Dr Redmond's lab book inside it.

If she looked behind her, she would see the twin paths of their footprints. She said, 'I think it happened yesterday. I think he must have been lying there all day.'

A quick glance. 'You can't be sure, Ellen. Best not to think about it.'

She shuddered, seeing him in her mind's eye, and put her hands to her face. Alec propped the bicycle against a lamp post and put his arms round her. She thought how shallow of her, how wrong, that a part of her was enjoying the warmth of his body, the murmur of his voice.

She stepped back. 'Sorry. Have you any more of that whisky, Alec?'

'Here.' They both drank from the flask. He said, 'Do you want to talk about it?'

'Not really.'

Not yet. There was something she needed to make up her mind about. Because she – and most likely only she – had overheard the quarrel between Dr Redmond and Dr Pharoah. *I could destroy you, you know. I've got proof and I'll use it, don't think that I won't.* And perhaps only hours later, Dr Redmond had died.

They reached the road. She managed to smile, looking at him. 'It must be – what, about twenty-five, twenty-six Fahrenheit? And you're not wearing any gloves.'

'I know. My mother would scold me. I forget them, you see.'

'Perhaps this doesn't seem cold to you.'

'Och, it's balmy. You're right, though, we can have some rough winters where I come from.'

'Where's that?'

'I live on an island called Seil. It's just off the west coast of Scotland, in Argyll, a wee bit south of Oban.'

'A big island or a small island?'

'A small island. And there's another even smaller island off it, called Easdale, where only a few dozen people live now.'

The feeling of being off-balance ebbed a little. She needed this interlude, cocooned in the frozen night, with its mingling of shock and desire and foreboding.

Alec said, 'My island's made of slate. My family used to quarry slate but the quarries are all disused now. In its heyday, slates from the islands were shipped all over the world.'

'How long have you lived there?'

'Och, I've always lived there. The Hunters have always lived there.'

'Martin called you the lord of the manor.'

'You don't want to believe everything Martin says. Our glory days are behind us. My great-great-grandfather built the house back in the middle of the last century. It's a nice old place. My forebears liked to add on another few rooms whenever they felt the need, and when I was a wee boy, I found out that you can get from one end of the building to the other through the attics and eaves. You can imagine that kept me amused for days.'

'Do you have any brothers and sisters?'

'No. My father died when I was thirteen, and afterwards there was only my mother and me. When my mother went out, I'd have the whole house to myself. Sometimes, it felt as if I had the whole island.'

'You must love it there.'

'Yes, I do.'

She thought he sounded sad. Odd, that, when you'd think such belonging would be a source of pride.

They reached the main road. She heard him sigh and say, 'And sometimes I hate it too, just a little. If you belong to a place like I do, you always have to keep going back. And then, how do you make yourself a future?'

She wondered whether the future he planned for himself had once included Andrée Fournier. And whether he had finished with Andrée or she had finished with him. She suspected the former. Perhaps Andrée was still in love with Alec Hunter. Perhaps she had been in love with him all along, and that was why she was so unhappy.

'Dr Redmond loved Peddar's Wood,' she said. 'He felt he belonged there. I wonder what will happen to it now.'

'Pharoah will sell it, I should think.'

She stared at him. His profile was a black silhouette against the dim, torch-lit night. 'The wood belongs to Dr Pharoah?'

'All that land does. It's Gildersleve land. And Pharoah's

short of money. You must have noticed the hall's held together by tin tacks and paste. Pharoah's overspent and even Alison's purse isn't bottomless. Or perhaps she doesn't choose to hand out the cash any more.'

'What do you mean?'

Alec shook his head. 'Nothing. Have you heard Martin's latest theory?'

He deflected the conversation neatly to work as they walked the rest of the way to Copfield. She knew that in walking her home, he was only being kind. Next day he would be distant again; next day she would be annoyed with herself again for hoping for more.

Riley and Superintendent Mildmay returned to Gildersleve Hall the following morning. In the soupy greyness of mid-December, the hall looked less impressive than it had the previous night. Riley noticed the chips in the stone steps that led up to the front door and the peeling paint on the window frames.

They spoke first to Dr Pharoah. Pharoah claimed grief at Redmond's death but Riley sensed beneath it anger and impatience. Then Riley interviewed the other employees of Gildersleve Hall while Mildmay remained with Pharoah.

Later, he tapped on the door of Ellen Kingsley's lab and went inside. Today she looked exhausted, barely holding it together. Riley wondered whether she had slept at all the previous night. She had a redhead's milk-coloured skin, but there were patches beneath her eyes that were bluish

81

and translucent, and the long, thin scratch across her cheek was as clear as a dark pen stroke on paper. Yet none of that altered the strong, unsettling attraction he felt towards her – unsettling because it was unexpected and unwished-for, and because it seemed to shine a glaring light on the threadbare nature of his feelings for Pearl.

There was another young woman in the room with Miss Kingsley – dark-haired, neatly pretty – who gave him a disapproving glare. Riley said, 'I apologize for disturbing you, Miss Fournier, Miss Kingsley. It was you I wanted to talk to, Miss Kingsley. Perhaps we could find somewhere.'

'Yes,' she said, and was out of the lab in two ticks, as if she couldn't wait to be free of the place.

On the landing, he said, 'Would you mind if we went to Dr Redmond's lab?'

'No, if you like.' Understandably, she didn't look keen. 'I'll get my coat, then. It's always freezing in there.'

She put on her coat and they went into the tower. 'I'm sorry about this,' he said to her when they were in the lab. He drew out a stool from beneath the bench. 'Sit down, please. I can see you'd rather not be here. But I find it hard to make sense of this place.'

'What do you mean?'

'How did he find anything?'

'I think he knew exactly where everything was. If you look carefully, you'll see that it isn't untidy, it's just cluttered. I think he was one of those men who collects things.'

'Stamps and tea cards?'

'And books and journals, and it doesn't look as if he ever threw away a piece of scientific equipment.'

'You see, when you said last night that you thought Dr Redmond's cottage had been searched, my superintendent's response was to ask how could you tell, because it was so untidy.'

'It had been searched, I'm sure of it.' She jutted out her chin. 'Dr Redmond hated things to be in a different place from where he'd put them.'

'Who might have searched it?'

'I don't know.'

He knew that she was holding something back. What was it? With long, tapering fingers she swept back a lock of hair that had fallen over her face, and said, 'When I went to the cottage last night, I noticed that there were no footprints in the snow. There was a snowfall on Monday night, so that means whoever searched it must have been and gone before then. Which means, I think, that Dr Redmond must have fallen down the stairs on Monday evening. And *that* means he'd lain there a whole day before I found him.' She looked upset.

'Because, you're saying, had he been able to, Dr Redmond would have tidied up?'

'Yes.'

'That does rather tie in with what we think about the time of death, I'm afraid.'

'It's funny,' she said, frowning. 'I don't have any convictions about life after death, none at all, so I don't think it can have made any difference to him, but it's still horrible to think of him all that time, lying there on his own.'

Tears glistened in her eyes; he sensed the effort she made to stop them falling. 'It's the last thing we can do for the people we've lost,' he said gently. 'Give them respect, keep a vigil. You were fond of Dr Redmond, weren't you, Miss Kingsley?'

'Yes, I was. He seemed so defenceless and so alone. But I don't know that he felt like that. And I shouldn't think he felt any fondness for me. I'm sure he never thought of me at all.' She stood up. 'If that's everything. I should get back to my work.'

'Yes, that's about it.' Riley watched her face as he said, 'Was it you who put Dr Redmond's lab book back?'

'Lab book?' He saw her go weak with shock and put out a hand to the bench.

'It wasn't there when I looked in here last night. I'm guessing it was either you or Mr Gosse who took it and put it back this morning. Or Alec Hunter, possibly. If it wasn't you, I'll go and talk to Gosse and Hunter about it.'

'It was me.'

'Why did you take it?'

She flopped on to the stool, resting her elbows on the bench, propping her head in her hands. 'I needed to check something.'

'You and your colleagues use these books to write up your work, don't you?'

'Yes, they're where we note down what we do on a day-to-day basis – experimental work, largely.'

'So you were trying to find out something about Dr Redmond's work?'

'In a way.' She paused, then said, 'A fortnight ago, Dr Redmond accused Dr Pharoah of plagiarism.'

'To his face?'

'No, he said it to me. That was why I took the book. I thought there might be something in it that would tell me what he'd meant.'

'And was there?'

'I don't think so. No, I really don't think so. And then . . .'

'Miss Kingsley?'

'They had an argument. Dr Redmond and Dr Pharoah. I overheard them.'

'When was that?'

'Monday afternoon. The day before yesterday.'

'Do you know what they were arguing about?'

'Not much. Some.'

He waited. She seemed to steel herself, as if about to take a big jump. 'Dr Redmond asked Dr Pharoah to leave him alone and Dr Pharoah said he wouldn't. Then Dr Redmond said that he could destroy Dr Pharoah, and that he had proof, and that he'd use it.'

'Those words exactly?'

'Pretty much.'

'What did he mean, proof? Proof of what?'

'I don't know. I've no idea. That was all I heard.' She

85

frowned. 'Dr Redmond sounded terribly upset. Furious, actually. And he was one of those people who are almost always on the same level.'

Pearl sometimes accused him of being like that. Since Annie's birth, Pearl's level had been all over the place.

A voice – Superintendent Mildmay's – called up the stairs, sharp-pitched and impatient. 'Inspector Riley? Are you up there?'

'He was upset,' said Miss Kingsley, giving him a direct look. 'People say things when they're upset, don't they?'

'They certainly do.' Riley gave her a smile, then went downstairs.

Inspector Riley was tall and broad-shouldered, with light brown hair parted to one side and patrician features: long nose, high forehead, firm jaw. Ellen had noticed the crackle of intelligence in his light hazel eyes when he had asked her about the book.

In telling him about the quarrel, she had made a conscious decision not to be one of Pharoah's men. The thought didn't make her feel proud of herself, or even frightened, just hazy with tiredness. And though she tried to tell herself that everything would be all right, she couldn't quite see how it could be. Inspector Riley would presumably ask Dr Pharoah about Dr Redmond's threat, because really, you could hardly ignore it, Dr Redmond saying he'd destroy Pharoah. And then, perhaps only hours later, dying.

The day seemed unnaturally long, too much waiting for

something to happen. She couldn't concentrate on her work and Andrée was still in a mood, so after a while she went downstairs to Alec Hunter's lab. She just slid in the door and sat on a stool and drank the coffee he made for her. She was glad he didn't talk much and she took a sharp pleasure watching him, the delicacy of his strong hands as they drew up liquid through a pipette, the small frown that settled on his forehead, the speed and clarity with which he worked. The moments passed, marked by the ticking of the clock and by the lightly falling snow outside, intimate, unvoiced.

Thursday morning: Dr Pharoah came to talk to them in the common room at break. The police were satisfied that Dr Redmond's death had been a tragic accident, Dr Pharoah told them. The coroner would make his report shortly and then the body would be released for burial. Dr Pharoah himself was making the arrangements as Dr Redmond had no close family. Unfortunately, Dr Pharoah would be absent in America at the time of the funeral – a long-standing engagement – but Dr Kaminski would represent him. He knew that there would be a strong turnout from Gildersleve Hall and his secretary would arrange the sending of flowers. Dr Redmond had been a brilliant scientist and a stalwart of Gildersleve Hall, part of the laboratory since its earliest days, and he would be greatly missed.

Pharoah left and people shuffled about. Toby and Jan

started up a chess game and Martin put the kettle on. So that's that, Ellen thought. Done and dusted. Someone, no doubt, would notice the striped mug still on the shelf and put it into a collection for a jumble sale. A new recruit would move into the lab in the tower.

Who searched your cottage? she thought. What were you and Pharoah quarrelling about? What proof had you meant to produce? Proof of what?

Martin said, 'Cheer up, Kingsley. Two weeks to go and then back home for jolly Christmas revelries.'

No one else saw anything troubling in Dr Redmond's death. No one else moved around the pieces in their heads, trying to fit them together.

They washed up their cups and left the common room. Martin walked upstairs with her. He'd had this cracker of an idea, he said, about the arrangement of inorganic ions in three dimensions. It had come to him at a party last night – yes, he knew, pretty bad form to go to a party when poor old Redmond was barely cold in his grave – well, not yet his grave, but she knew what he meant – but he'd had to get away from all the gloom, it was giving him the heebie-jeebies.

They went into the lab. Andrée wasn't there. It was a little warmer today; Ellen wiped the condensation from a windowpane and became still, looking down to the bike shed. A flash of red scarf, a dark mop of curls, and Alec's hand on the back of Andrée's neck, bending her head towards him. They kissed, she thought with a flood of pain, as if they were the only people in the world. As if it was the only thing to do in the world.

Ellen had not noticed Martin coming to stand beside her. He whistled. 'Crikey. Well, well, well. I *wondered* whether that was starting up again.' He glanced at her. 'I take it you had no idea?'

'No,' she whispered.

'I saw them together in Cambridge a few days ago. I'd have filled you in but we'd had our little tiff.'

You thought you understood but then you discovered that you were completely wrong. You had hopes, however unfounded or irrational, and then something forced you to put them aside.

After Martin had left the room, Ellen sat down at the bench, opened her lab book and unscrewed her pen. She wrote the date, underlined it, then put down the pen, put her hands over her face, and wept.

On Friday evening, as Riley was about to leave work, Ellen Kingsley phoned him at Cambridge police station.

After saying hello and apologizing for interrupting him, she dived in. 'Dr Pharoah told us that the police think Dr Redmond's death was an accident,' she said. 'Is that what you believe, Inspector Riley?'

Sergeant Claybrooke put a sheaf of papers on his desk. Riley nodded thanks. He said, 'Cause of death was a broken neck, Miss Kingsley. There was a rip in the carpet at the top of the stairs and strands of carpet had stuck to one of

Redmond's shoes, which was damp. So yes, it seems likely that his death was an unfortunate accident. The coroner will make the final verdict, of course.'

'Did anyone try to find out who'd searched the cottage?'

'I interviewed both Dr Pharoah and Roy Gosse. They claimed to know nothing about it.'

'So you're just ignoring it, not bothering.' She sounded furious.

He said, 'Where are you, Miss Kingsley?'

'I'm in a phone box in Copfield.'

Copfield was south-west of Cambridge, on his way home, more or less. Riley slid the papers into his briefcase. 'I was about to set off for London. I could stop in at the Green Man if you like. Would you mind waiting fifteen minutes or so for me?'

'No, of course not.' Some of the anger melted from her voice. 'Thank you.'

As he drove out of Cambridge he wondered what impulse had led him to suggest meeting Ellen Kingsley. It occurred to him that he was putting off going home because he wanted to extend his last few days' respite from the stormy unpredictability of his marriage.

In the private bar of the Green Man an elderly couple were sitting in a corner, the man with a beer, the woman drinking something with a cherry in it. Apart from them, Ellen Kingsley was the only other person in the room. She was wearing a green jersey over a white shirt, and her hair, which she wore tied back at work, tumbled loose to her shoulders.

Catching sight of him, she said, 'Thank you for coming, Inspector. I appreciate it.'

'John,' he said. 'Or Riley, if you prefer.' He gave a wry smile. 'There are always a great many Johns, so I've tended to stick with Riley. May I get you another drink, Miss Kingsley?'

'Ellen,' she said. 'A whisky and ginger, please.' His concern must have showed because she added, rather irritably, 'I'm not getting plastered, if that's what you're thinking. My father taught me how to appreciate a good Scotch. And I seem to feel cold all the time and it warms me up.'

'That's shock,' he told her. 'It can take a few days to set in.'

He bought the drinks. Sitting down opposite her, he said, 'Isn't it most likely that it was Redmond himself who'd searched the cottage? Perhaps you're right, perhaps he had fallen out with Pharoah. And perhaps he thought he had something to use against Pharoah but couldn't find it in all the clutter. Perhaps he was looking for whatever it was, went upstairs, searched the bedroom, tripped on the torn carpet and fell.'

'The photographs,' she said obstinately. 'There were photographs of Peddar's Wood all over on the floor. I don't think Dr Redmond loved many human beings, but he did love that wood. He wouldn't have just chucked the photos on the floor.'

'People don't always act rationally when they're angry. As for the accusation of plagiarism, isn't it possible that Dr Redmond was mistaken, or exaggerating?'

She threaded her hands together, her brow creased. 'I wondered about that. It's not always as easy as outsiders sometimes think, knowing who's responsible for a discovery. It's not always – not even usually – some experiment showing something amazing and someone crying eureka. Most scientific advances are collaborative. Someone finds a piece of the jigsaw and someone else finds another and so on. Most of the time, you're working long hours on your own. Maybe the strain was telling on Dr Redmond.'

While she talked, Riley found himself distracted by the planes and shadows of her face and the way that the fire-light cast two flickers of golden light into her grey eyes. He asked, 'Do two scientists ever come up with the same theory at the same time?'

'Yes, even when they're working separately. It can be very competitive, scientific research. But there's a sort of unspoken agreement – a gentlemen's agreement – that if one scientist is working on a particular field of research then the others will leave him to it and concentrate on something else.'

'Is Dr Pharoah a gentleman?'

Sidestepping his question, Ellen said, 'If you'd been working away at something for years, and if you were pipped at the post, you might think you'd been cheated of all the glory. But it wouldn't necessarily be true. But when Dr Redmond used the word "proof", I thought at the time he meant something solid, something written.'

'Why?'

'I don't know. No, I really don't know. I suppose because he was that sort of man. Factual, literal. But maybe I got the wrong end of the stick. Maybe I shouldn't have said anything about the quarrel. Maybe I've been foolish – and disloyal.' She looked utterly miserable.

'You wanted us to find out the truth about what had happened to your friend. There's nothing foolish or disloyal in that. I'm sure Dr Pharoah will have understood that you had no alternative but to tell us what you'd heard.'

Yet he spoke with a confidence he did not feel. He had recognized something slippery in Gildersleve's director. Riley had not taken to Marcus Pharoah. And Superintendent Mildmay's rushed tidying up and skimping of procedure to protect Pharoah's reputation had left a sour taste in his mouth.

'There's something that struck me as curious.' As he glanced through his notebook, Riley heard a roar from the public bar. 'Bryan David Jeffrey Redmond . . . Did brilliantly at school, went to Cambridge when he was only seventeen, was awarded a double first. His father died while he was still at school, his mother passed away at the end of the war. He had no brothers, sisters or cousins and no one I spoke to could tell me of any friends. Yet I found old train tickets in his house. Tickets to London.'

'I saw him once, getting off the train at King's Cross.'

'I checked up at Cambridge station and the clerk and

guard remembered seeing him every month. He went to London regularly as clockwork, going back years. My sergeant found a stack of tickets in the cottage, both overground and underground. Odd dates on them.'

She pressed her thumb knuckle against her teeth. 'You have to give your return ticket in at the barrier. Presumably Dr Redmond only kept his when it was busy and the ticket inspector didn't get the chance to look at his ticket. That would explain the odd dates.'

'Why would he keep the tickets?'

'I told you, because he was a hoarder.'

'Do you have any idea what Dr Redmond might have been doing in London?'

'I'm afraid not.'

'Visiting a friend, perhaps. Or a lover.'

'A lover?' She smiled. 'No.'

'Most people have secrets, Miss Kingsley. I do. I expect you do too.'

She flushed, then looked away, and he realized that he had touched a nerve. She wore no ring on her finger, but was she attached to someone, secretly or otherwise? Someone, perhaps, at Gildersleve Hall?

She said, 'All those things you've just told me about Dr Redmond, I hardly knew any of them. I didn't even know he was called Bryan. That's rather sad, isn't it?' She gave a small shake of the head. 'Have you ever felt bored by your own thoughts, Riley?'

'Frequently.'

'Mine aren't getting me anywhere at all. I keep thinking I should have gone to him. On Monday afternoon, after the quarrel, I should have gone to him. He wouldn't have wanted me to, but still.'

'I doubt if it would have made any difference. He doesn't sound the sort of man to whom confidences came easily.' Riley glanced at his watch. 'I should head off, my wife and daughter will be expecting me. May I give you a lift to your lodgings?'

'Are you trying to make sure I don't sit here drinking all evening?' she said with a mocking lift of the eyebrows. But she rose and he helped her on with her coat.

As they left the pub, two men were hauling Roy Gosse out of the public bar. Forcibly ejected into the street, Gosse tumbled into the snow, cursing. Riley took Ellen's elbow to steer her out of the way.

On the short drive to her lodgings on the Cambridge road they spoke little. Outside the bungalow, Riley parked, wrote on a page from his notebook, tore it off and gave it to her. 'This will be my London number,' he said. 'I'll be transferring back to the Met shortly. Do please give me a ring if anything comes up. But for what it's worth, I think Dr Redmond slipped and fell downstairs. And not just because Mildmay and Pharoah prefer it that way.'

Miss Kingsley nodded, and climbed out of the car. Riley waited until she had opened the front door and gone inside the bungalow. Then he put the car into gear and drove away.

*   *   *

The new house, a pleasant, if shabby, four-bedroomed townhouse, was in Tufnell Park, in north London. When Riley arrived home at half past nine, Pearl was standing at the living-room window, smoking.

She said, 'Where were you?' and he felt his heart sink.

'Working.' He took off his coat and scarf. 'And the traffic was bad coming into London. Is Annie asleep?'

'She was tired, out like a light by seven.'

Pearl was wearing her old Chinese dressing gown, shiny red with embroidered dragons, over a pair of slacks and a purple jersey. She was tall and thin and had long black hair, a white skin and pale green eyes.

She flicked ash on to a saucer. 'I thought you'd be back ages ago.'

'The hours are going to be longer than usual until I'm back at Scotland Yard. I thought I explained that.'

A mistake, that last phrase. Her beautiful face contorted and she said, 'You could have been anywhere. You could have been with anyone.'

'But I wasn't.' The fact that he was, strictly speaking, lying, made him add quickly, 'Look, I'm here now. How was your day?'

'Awful. I don't know where anything is and the hall light's not working, and I can't get the fire to light and I'm freezing.' Pearl's long, thin fingers were working at the folds of her kimono. 'It's all right for you, you can just go off, but I'm stuck here all day. And there's a funny noise in the airing cupboard.'

'There's probably air in the pipes.'

'What if it's mice? I hate mice! Christ, John!'

He put his arms round her and held her until she stopped trembling. 'I'll have a look in the airing cupboard,' he said, as he stroked her spine. 'Have you eaten anything?'

'Toast with Annie.'

'I'll make us something. OK?'

'OK.' She took a gasping breath and got herself under control. Then she nodded. 'Sorry, John.'

He lit the fire then went to the kitchen, where he scratched together a tea from the meagre supplies in the larder. Cardboard boxes of saucepans and utensils were scattered around the room, and, as Pearl had said, nothing was in the right place. While a tin of soup was warming he went upstairs to check on their daughter.

Annie was four years old. She had wavy brown hair and green eyes like Pearl's. She was fast asleep in bed, her limbs flung out in a starfish shape. Riley tucked her in, kissed her and went back downstairs.

They ate in the living room, in front of the fire. Then Pearl made herself a hot-water bottle and went up to bed. Riley found a torch and had a good look in the airing cupboard, then stuck his head round the bedroom door to reassure her that there was no sign of mice.

'I suppose you think I'm imagining it,' she said and turned away from him, pulling the eiderdown over her head.

As he went downstairs he felt a sense of relief settle over

him. This was an emotion that he was familiar with, and which came upon him as soon as Pearl had gone to bed or had left the house, bringing an end to accusations and tears on her part, and to his own tiptoeing around her moods. But tonight his relief was fleeting. He felt short-changed, aware of a mixture of resentment and despair.

He had met Pearl at a north London bus stop in the spring of 1944. Their attraction had been instant and flammable, their affair all-consuming and passionate, enacted against a dreary, dangerous wartime background. By the time he had flown to Normandy three weeks later with the D-Day landing force, he and Pearl had become engaged. During the Allied armies' slow progress north through France in the summer and autumn of 1944, and then across a snow-swept Belgium and Germany into spring, he had treasured her letters and his memory of her.

At last, after almost six years of war, peace had come. After a stint in the military police in Berlin, Riley had been discharged at the end of 1946. He had returned to London, where Pearl had been waiting for him, and where their wedding was to take place a week after his homecoming. It had taken him only a day to discover that during their two and a half year parting, something had changed. She had been the same, but he had altered. He had found her wild happiness, which had formerly entranced him, disturbing, and her sudden swings from elation to dejection, which had once seemed characterful and exciting, had jarred.

Yet there had never been a moment during which he

considered voicing his reservations, or altering the future that lay before him. He had made his promises and must keep them. He had grown too used to solitariness, he told himself, and to army life. Love would return.

But it had not. The day-to-day realities of marriage, set against a cheerless post-war London, had ground down any fond, lingering memories of their three-week love affair. The succession of rented flats they had lived in before they were able to buy a house, the shortages and rationing and the appalling weather of the winter of 1947–48 would have tested the most close-knit couple. And they were not close-knit; he could neither soothe her anxieties nor satisfy her longings, and she in turn quickly found his long hours at work trying, his steadiness irksome.

A year after they had married Pearl had fallen pregnant with Annie. She had been well enough throughout the pregnancy, but soon after the birth had fallen into a deep depression. A doctor had prescribed pills and somehow they had managed. Pearl's mother, Vera, had helped with Annie, who, thankfully, had been an easy baby, easy to care for and so easy to love. Pearl's recovery had been slow and stuttering, a few steps forward followed by a backward slide into silence and sadness. There had been the added burden of trying to hide her illness from other people. Riley knew the sorts of words his colleagues used. *Nuts. Batty. A screw loose.*

It had been Pearl who had seized on the idea of the move to the countryside, partly for the fields and fresh air

– so good for Annie – and partly to make a new start. Fields and fresh air were only pleasurable in the summer, however, and she had quickly found the winters long and cold and lacking in diversion. Less than two years later, she had clamoured with equal fervour to return to London. Though Riley welcomed the move and his return to the Metropolitan Police, his thoughts drifted back to the frosty, pared-down landscape of Cambridgeshire.

And then to Ellen Kingsley. He considered her rational demeanour, her intelligence and composure, her humour. He remembered her calm grey eyes and the fall of her dark red hair. Admit it, Riley, you wanted to meet Ellen in the pub in Copfield because you wanted to see her one last time.

He had known he should not, and that afterwards he would regret it. He regretted it because half an hour in her company had shown him what might have been. Now, unpacking boxes in the kitchen, he paused for a moment, remembering the short drive from the pub to her lodgings, remembering the silence of the snowy landscape and the deep, bittersweet pleasure he had felt in being close to her.

They buried Dr Redmond in the churchyard in Copfield on a chill, windless day, and afterwards drank to his memory in the Green Man. The snow thawed, leaving puddles beside the bare hedgerows. At Gildersleve, the secretaries decorated the tree in the hall and put up paper chains. A grey, wet Christmas heaved itself closer.

Ellen went with Toby and Martin to a review in

Cambridge. Toby's girlfriend, Lise, whom he had met through his cycling club, joined them. Joe visited and they caught a train to the coast and walked along the shingle beach at Dunwich.

Dr Pharoah was still away in Boston. Ellen's relationship with Andrée was as it had always been, civil and distant, and Ellen avoided Alec Hunter. Perhaps the affair had started up again weeks ago. Perhaps Alec and Andrée had been lovers all the time that she, Ellen, had been foolish enough to begin to think that he liked her.

As for Bryan Redmond, it seemed to her that Inspector Riley's interpretation of events had probably been right. Pharoah's career had overtaken Dr Redmond's during the war. You could see how it might have happened: Pharoah the talker and the charmer, Dr Redmond hardly able to look you in the eye. Someone had to make their way through the committees and grant boards, someone had to say the right things to the right people, and that person would never have been Dr Redmond. Perhaps it wasn't what you had seen yourself doing, the bureaucracy and the toadying, but if you had a dream like Marcus Pharoah's, the price was worth paying.

It was possible Dr Redmond had never accepted the acceleration of Pharoah's career. Perhaps it had rankled, fuelling resentment that had built up over the years. Wanting to humble Pharoah, he had gone back to the cottage to try to find something, anything, that would hurt him, and in doing so had slipped and fallen to his death. And she, too, had stumbled, clumsy and cack-handed, blundering over desires and secrets she had not fully understood, blurting out misconceived notions when she would have done better to keep quiet.

She felt as if she moved precariously, stepping around other people's jealousies and broken dreams. She longed for Christmas, longed to go home. And then, in the New Year, she could return to Gildersleve Hall and begin again.

The evening before she was due to leave Gildersleve, Ellen packed her case for home. A layer of shoes, books and Christmas presents at the bottom of her case, then skirts, cardigans and blouses folded over them, underwear and stockings tucked round the sides. She was to take the train to London after work the next day; her father would meet her at King's Cross. A table was booked in a restaurant where Joe would join them, and they would spend the night in a hotel before taking the train to Wiltshire the following morning.

There was an end-of-term atmosphere at the hall the next day, people giving out Christmas cards, tidying up, writing up notes, or rushing from one floor to another, trying to find belongings that had been lent or lost. Dr Pharoah must have returned to England because his Jaguar was parked in the courtyard. Ellen heard his voice now and then, rich and mellifluous, from a lower floor.

At mid-afternoon, she went to the common room. Toby and Jan Kaminski were playing chess; one of the researchers from the 'beta' group was looking over Toby's shoulder, sucking his teeth in a disapproving manner whenever a move was made.

Dr Padfield was making punch in a chemical flask over a camping stove. Martin said, 'God, the stink, Padders, what the hell have you put in there?'

'Brandy and cloves. And my secret ingredient.'

'Snake venom . . .'

'Castor oil.'

'Who's coming to the pub later?'

'Some of us have families to go home to, Finch.'

The door opened and Dr Pharoah came in.

'Punch, Pharoah?' said Padfield.

'Thank you, Paddy, but no.'

'How was America?'

'An excellent trip. Some fascinating stuff. Let's have a drink one evening, Bill, and I'll fill you in. Jan, do you have those notes I asked you for?'

Jan Kaminski stood up. 'They're in my office.'

'Thank you. I have the Medical Research Council breathing down my neck.' Pharoah went to the door. 'Enjoy your holiday, gentlemen, and I look forward to seeing everyone in the New Year.' Then he turned to Ellen. 'When you have finished your tea, Miss Kingsley, please come to my office.'

Pharoah left the room. It was all just the same, the cloves-and-oranges smell of the punch, the click of cup and saucer, and the 'beta' group scientist sliding into Jan Kaminski's seat as Toby moved a piece on the chessboard.

103

But inside Ellen, something had solidified, leaden and knotted, and it was all she could do to swallow another mouthful of tea and take her cup and saucer to the sink.

In the cloakroom, she pulled a comb through her hair and checked her face in the mirror. Then she knocked on the door of Dr Pharoah's office.

And then he was calling her to come in and beckoning her to sit down, and he was telling her that things had not worked out as he would have hoped, that he was sorry, and he was sure she would find some other niche more suited to her abilities, but he must regretfully inform her that he did not wish her to return to Gildersleve Hall after Christmas. And all the while he looked at her with executioner's eyes, dark and ruthless, as he let the axe fall.

Ellen rested her forehead against the windowpane in the lab. Rain battered against the glass and she closed her eyes.

'You're leaving?' said Andrée.

'Yes.'

'When?'

'Now, I think.' She moved from the window and swept things from her desk into her briefcase: notebooks, a slide rule, sandwich tin.

'Oh, Ellen.'

So this was it, this was the beginning. Pity and shock and disapproval and maybe a little gloating: she would have to endure them all.

She went to the box room and put on her coat. Andrée

had followed her out of the lab. She said, 'How could he?' and, 'This is so *wrong*,' and then suddenly, unexpectedly, crushing Ellen's hand in hers, hugged her. 'Perhaps you've had a lucky escape.'

People were leaving the hall, calling out farewells. Ellen's legs felt unsteady as she went downstairs, and she kept a hand on the banister for support. Just then she could quite see how, giddy with shock, you might lose your balance and fall. Another flight of stairs, then she crossed the hall. Outside, rain fell from a dense grey sky.

Ahead of her on the path, Alec Hunter was going to the bike shed; she stood back in the lee of the outhouse, out of sight in the dim tunnel of honeysuckle tendrils and old man's beard, waiting till he had gone. She heard the percussive beat of Gosse chopping up wood and the bark of the dog as it ran round the kitchen garden. She watched Alec cross the path in front of her; she thought he might hear the beating of her heart, but he did not, and she clenched her fists, pressing her knuckles against her teeth. What would she tell her family? What would she say to her father? How would she endure the dust and ashes of the meal that night, which was meant to be a celebration?

Her sense of shame and of failure was so intense at that moment that it was hard to carry on. Her briefcase slid out of her hand and she leaned against the wall of the building for support. But the cool air revived her and drops of water fell on her face, and after a while she picked up her case and stumbled on.

Part Two

London

1954–1956

Chapter Three

Because she was a lot messier than Sebastian, India had the bedroom. Sebastian slept on the sitting-room sofa, folding and tidying away his bedding each morning. His clothes, a rather sparse collection, one of everything for best and one of everything for gardening, hung in the wardrobe, looking faded and uncertain next to India's frocks, which seemed to have a life of their own, slipping off hangers and edging out of the door, preventing it from shutting, as if they disliked being enclosed in the darkness.

The flat had belonged to Aunt Rachel, who had rescued them. This was how India always thought of it, rescued, with no inverted commas. When they had first come to the flat, Aunt Rachel had given India and Sebastian the bedroom and she herself had slept on the sofa. India had slept in Aunt Rachel's bed and Sebastian had had a camp bed, though he had often crawled in with India during the night. As they had grown older, Aunt Rachel had bought a folding screen from an antique shop and had put it up between India's and Sebastian's beds, to give them some privacy, she said. The screen was made out of something called découpage and was covered with pictures that looked as if they had been cut out from magazines, ladies in bonnets or holding parasols, and big-eyed, pink-cheeked children.

India tried on all her evening frocks and eventually settled for a white satin one she had found at Berwick Street Market. She dressed it up with a spray of cobalt-blue flowers, made of paper stiffened with wax, pinned to the neckline. Always accessorize, her mother used to say, peering short-sightedly into a mirror as she threaded earrings into her lobes. A dozen dresses lay on the bed; others had fallen to the floor, so that the room was filled with glorious splashes of powder blue and coral and buttercup yellow. The colours reminded India of the art supply shop in Piccadilly where she worked. Of all the jobs she had ever had, it was by far her most favourite. She liked the smell of the shop, a mixture of wax and linseed oil and paper. Pastels and watercolours nestled inside boxes beneath fragile tissue paper coverings, graded in rainbow colours from white to black. The names printed on the paper wrappings were as beautiful as the blocks of paint themselves: vermilion, cerise, ultramarine and turquoise.

The shop also stocked papers for bookbinding, swirled with amber and maroon and peacock blue like the frozen ripples of a river. Customers came into the shop and bought a sheet of marbled paper or a five-pint can of turpentine and a fine sable brush. India had met her boyfriend, Garrett, at the shop. Garrett wasn't an artist; he had been looking for cartridge paper to make posters to advertise a jazz band. He represented the jazz band, which sounded rather glamorous, though in time India had discovered that what Garrett actually did was to tramp around pubs and clubs, trying to persuade their owners to let the band play there.

Garrett Parker was twenty-three, a year older than India. He came from a small town in Leicestershire ('the sticks'). He was of medium height, muscular, black-haired, dark-eyed and olive-skinned, and he had a charming, mischievous grin. People sometimes thought he was Italian. India knew that Garrett, who had an eye for nice things, liked the contrast they made, she as fair as a wheatfield, he dark and foreign-looking. She didn't mind it herself, thought they looked pretty good together. That morning, in bed, she had tried to lie still so as not to wake Garrett, who had been sleeping beside her, but after a couple of minutes she had become bored and had wriggled round and kissed him. His eyelids had fluttered and his lashes had brushed against hers, like moths colliding near a candle flame. Then their bodies had locked together, finding familiar and favourite places before either of them said a word.

Garrett had a lot of different jobs. As well as the jazz band, he looked after half a dozen flats for a friend of his, repairing them and collecting the rent. He also bought and sold antiques. Aunt Rachel, who had known about antiques, would have called them junk, but Garrett loved his chipped creamware and amateurish oil paintings. ('Lovely piece. I'll hang on to it till it appreciates.' Garrett's flat was full of things waiting to appreciate.) Now and then, Garrett delivered cars to garages or private homes in far-flung parts of the country. A couple of times India had gone with him, once to a huge mansion in Chester, and another time to a garage in Southampton. On the Southampton trip, she had wondered, as they drove through Hampshire, whether they might come across the house in the woods. She had thought of mentioning it to Garrett, but hadn't, partly because she couldn't remember where exactly it had been, and partly because she found it hard to believe that it still existed – or whether, indeed, it had existed at all. In her memory, it was like a dream. Or a nightmare.

India sat down at the dressing table. Her hair, which was up in rollers, was thick and slightly curly, platinum blond. People thought she bleached it but she didn't, just rinsed it in lemon juice so that it kept its straw-stubble whiteness. Looking into the mirror, she pursed her lips and narrowed her blue eyes into a sultry expression. Her own image looked back at her, dreamy, beckoning. People – men – told her she was beautiful, but she couldn't always see it. Sometimes she looked in the mirror and thought, yes, you'll do, but at other times her face seemed to her as bland and featureless as a suet pudding, an empty space dotted with holes for eyes, mouth, nostrils.

India blobbed foundation on to a sponge and rubbed it into her skin. Then powder, forcing the puff into the crevices of her compact to get out the last crumbly bits and working it into the contours of cheek and chin and finishing off with quick little dabs. Leaning closer to the mirror (she had inherited her mother's short-sightedness) she drew a thin black line along each lid, flicking it up at the corners. Then she spat in her mascara, scrubbed it with the tiny brush and blackened her lashes. Eyebrow pencil, a dark red lipstick, and then she took the rollers out of her hair, scowling as they caught and pulled. She put the discarded rollers on to the dressing table, where they jostled, pink bristly plastic, with the bottles of make-up and perfume and the bracelets and tissues. She ran a comb through her hair: the curl had gone and it lay on her shoulders, as smooth and pale as the white satin dress.

She lit a cigarette and went to the window. The bedroom looked out to the back of the house, over the garden. Rachel's flat – she still thought of it as Rachel's flat, though Rachel herself had died six years ago – was in a street off Tottenham Court Road. One of the houses opposite had been struck by a bomb in the war and India remembered coming home in the school holidays and seeing the gap and the rubble and the dust. A garage had been built in the gap, though an area of wasteland still existed to one side of it. India watched as a big silver car glided into the forecourt of the garage. A boy came out of the kiosk and put petrol in the tank and wiped a cloth over the car's windscreen. A bus stopped at the near side of the road and half a dozen passengers, the women loaded with shopping bags and the men carrying a newspaper or a briefcase, climbed out. The queue of people moved up as those at the front squeezed on to the bus.

Each of the gardens visible from the window of the flat had its own character. There was the messy one, with a rusty pram and dun-coloured armchairs with holes in the seats, and the tidy one, mostly lawn, daffodils in the borders. In India's favourite garden a wisteria covered the back wall; in a month or so its flowers would hang like lilac grapes. The garden of India's and Sebastian's house was owned by the couple in the ground floor flat. They had two children, whose toys – a tricycle, a ball and dolls – were scattered over the grass. The line was full of washing, and India watched, unfocused, as the stockings, bras, vests, pants and girdles flicked in the breeze.

She turned away and scrabbled in the mess at the bottom of the wardrobe until she found a pale blue chiffon scarf, which she tied over her hair. Then she collected her coat and handbag and went outside.

Eight hours later, the white satin dress was on the floor of Garrett's room. India herself was lying on Garrett's fold-down bed. You either lay on the flat piece that formed the seat when the bed was a sofa, and whose springs stabbed you in the back, or you slid one way or the other on the rounded upper section. India had chosen the springs. She was naked and cold – Garrett's room ('my flat') was always cold – but she liked the way the lamplight made her look like a marble statue.

Garrett's flat was long and thin, part of a single large room that had been cut in half with a plywood partition. Each room could hear most of what went on in the other, so India and Garrett only went to bed when Ronnie was out. This was at India's insistence; Garrett, who was a show-off, couldn't have cared less what Ronnie heard. Apart from the fold-down bed there was a table and two chairs, a gas ring, a shelf with packets of coffee and food, a record player, radio and a wooden clothes horse, on which Garrett kept his shirts and trousers. His leather jacket hung on a peg on the door.

Garrett was walking around, no clothes on, making coffee. Garrett was even vainer than India was. He did indeed have a very nice body; when she had first seen him in the shop, she had fallen in love with the set of his shoulders and the swell of his forearm, flecked with black hairs.

Spooning instant into a cup, he said, 'Taking a car to Plymouth on Sunday. Do you want to come?'

'I can't.'

'Go on, Indy, it's be fun. We could go to the beach.'

'It's Sebastian's birthday. He's eighteen on Sunday.' India rolled on to her side. 'I need to buy him a present.'

'I found a lovely little painting the other day.' Garrett

picked up a small framed picture that was propped against the wall and showed it to her. 'It'd clean up nicely.'

India doubted it. It was hard to tell what the painting represented, the oils were so dark: the inside of a cave, perhaps, or the bottom of the sea. 'I don't think Sebastian's very keen on art,' she said tactfully. 'I thought I might buy him some books.'

'Good idea.'

'But I'm awfully short of cash.'

Garrett put the coffee on the table and sat down beside her on the edge of the bed. She rolled on to her back again and he ran his hand, warm from holding the mug, over her belly. 'Me, too, I'm afraid, darlin'. Oliver's promised me a cut of the takings tonight, but I expect it'll be weeks till I see any of it.'

She sighed. 'I wish I was rich.'

'I'm going to be rich one day, Indy. One day soon.'

'Maybe I'll marry a millionaire,' she said, teasing him.

'Bernie's going to be at the club tomorrow night. It's his birthday. Are you coming?'

'I don't like Bernie.'

'Bernie's a jerk, but the club's good fun and he'll be buying the drinks.' The pad of Garrett's thumb scooped out the curve of her waist. 'You've got goose pimples.'

'So have you.'

'Better warm us up, then.'

She gave a little yawn and arched her body, stretching her arms over her head. 'I suppose so.'

116

'You *suppose* so?' He sat up, made a sound that might have been outrage and might have been lust, then scooped her up in his arms, dumped her on his knee, and began to kiss her.

In a bookshop the next day, India chose for Sebastian a Hornblower and a John Creasey and tucked them under her raincoat. Then she thought that Sebastian might find the John Creasey too gruesome, so she put it back and went instead to browse the gardening section. Apart from the owner, who was sitting at the till, there were only two other people in the bookshop, a young woman and an old man. The young woman was on the opposite side of the shop, her back to India, and the old man had come in to escape the rain and wasn't even pretending to read.

India found a nice book about roses. The shopkeeper had dropped her glasses on the floor and was scrabbling under the table to retrieve them, so India slipped the book beneath her raincoat and went outside.

It was still raining. She heard the shop door open behind her, and her stomach squeezed. She didn't want to have to run for it, she was wearing high heels and she hated to be shouted at. In the seconds before she noticed that it wasn't the owner who had come out of the shop but the young woman, stories ran through her head: a sick grandmother who adored gardening, or amnesia, perhaps.

The young woman was wearing a fawn mackintosh and she had red hair, and she was looking at India in a determined – and reproving – way.

India peered at her. Then she said, 'Ellen. Oh, Ellen, it is you, isn't it?'

'Good Lord,' said the red-haired woman, staring at her. 'India Mayhew.'

'How wonderful to see you again.' India felt a bubble of happiness rise up inside her.

'And you,' said Ellen, which delighted India, though she sensed politeness.

There was a certain look in Ellen's eyes, which India remembered, so she said quickly, 'You won't tell, will you? They're not for me, they're for Sebastian.'

Ellen frowned. 'But India, you can't just *take* things.'

This made India think of school. But India, you can't just do whatever you want. When all she had suggested was nipping off the school premises or faking a headache to get out of games.

She said, 'It's Sebastian's birthday and I haven't enough money.'

'Then I'll lend you the money and you can pay me back.'

India chewed her lip. She felt cornered. 'I can't go back in,' she muttered.

'Just say you forgot to pay.'

'That woman looks such a dragon. She'll be cross with me.'

118

'Here, give me the books.' Ellen's expression was one that India was familiar with, a mixture of exasperation and resignation.

Ellen took the books and went inside. When she came out of the shop a few minutes later, they were in a brown paper bag, which she handed to India.

'And you mustn't do it again,' she said.

'I won't, I promise. Never, ever. You must come to tea. I live just round the corner.'

'There's no need.'

'It's the least I can do,' said India, becoming her most gracious. Her mother had used to say, good manners don't cost anything, which was perfectly true, and something India had always remembered and tried to emulate. 'You must come, Ellen,' she said. 'Then you can meet Sebastian.' She beamed at Ellen. 'It's so lovely to see you. I always knew we'd meet again. I had a *feeling*.'

India Mayhew lived a short walk from the bookshop. Her flat was on the second floor of a terraced house. The sitting room was small and pleasant and looked out over the back garden. It was immaculate, the cushions plumped up, a small pile of books and magazines neatly arranged. The ornaments on the mantelpiece – a Dresden shepherdess, Clarice Cliff jug and Venetian glass paperweight – were lined up equidistantly from each other.

'Sebastian,' called India.

A boy of eighteen or so came out of another room.

119

India said, 'Ellen, this is my brother Sebastian. Seb, this is Ellen Kingsley. She's an old friend of mine.'

Well, thought Ellen, I wouldn't have put it quite like that. But she said, 'Hello, Sebastian. I'm very pleased to meet you.'

Sebastian Mayhew was slight, not particularly tall, and his curling hair was a darker blond than India's. His eyes were blue, like his sister's, his features regular and classical, and his smile was incomparably sweet. He was the sort of boy, Ellen thought, to whom you would always give a second and third glance, because he was strikingly beautiful. India was beautiful too, and had the same sweet smile, but she had not that aura of goodness about her.

'Ellen was at Hayfields with me,' said India.

'P-pleased to meet you, Ellen,' said Sebastian. 'S-schools are frightful places, aren't they?'

'Your school wasn't frightful.' India explained to Ellen, 'They didn't have to do any maths or anything horrible at Sebastian's school, just woodwork and gardening.'

'Woodwork and gardening are very useful,' said Ellen.

'I think so,' said Sebastian. 'Would you like a scone? I've just made some.'

They ate scones and drank tea at the kitchen table. India talked constantly, about her job in a shop, her friends and a film she had seen. Ellen remembered that India had never been one for silences. Sebastian was quiet; Ellen wondered whether he couldn't get a word in or whether his slight stutter put him off talking. Though now she came to think of it, India, too, had had an occasional stutter at school, which had tended to come on in moments of stress, when she was at a loss or being told off.

India said, 'What about you, Ellen? Where do you live?'

'In a house in Islington. I share with my brother, Joe, and some of his friends. Joe's an engineering student. I work in a hospital in St Pancras Way, so it's not too far from work.'

'So both of us share flats with our brothers!' exclaimed India delightedly, as if this was something extraordinary. 'I'd love to meet your brother. And Sebastian would too.'

'Well,' said Sebastian. He had eaten a scone, very tidily. Ducking his head, he said, 'I should go and see Florence. I haven't been round for a week and she was worried about Arthur. Goodbye, Ellen, it's been super meeting you.'

'Sebastian gardens for lots of old ladies,' explained India to Ellen, after the door had closed behind her brother. 'They all feed him pieces of cake. If I ate as much cake as Sebastian does I'd be very fat, but he walks everywhere because he doesn't like the Tube, and then there's all the gardening, so he's always as thin as a rake. Me and my boyfriend are going out for a drink. Would you like to come with us?'

Startled by the abrupt change of subject, Ellen said, 'I don't think so, thank you. I shouldn't think your boyfriend would want me hanging around.'

'Oh, Garrett would adore meeting you, I know he would. You could have supper here and I could lend you a lovely dress and then we could all go out together.'

Ellen was remembering how India sucked you into her life. You didn't mean to succumb, but somehow it happened. 'I'm afraid I've something on,' she said. 'Another time, perhaps.' She glanced at her watch. 'I'd better go.'

'Must you?'

'Things to do . . . It's been lovely to see you again, India.'

India presented her with a piece of paper and a pencil. 'You must write down your address so I can pay you back for the books.' Ellen was aware of tides turning, storms brewing.

She took a bus back to Islington, sitting on the top deck with the smokers. The seats were crowded, but a woman with two small boys hauled them both on to her lap so that Ellen could sit down. The boys were each given a Spangle, which they unwrapped with careful concentration.

The bus shuddered away from the stop, passing a magnolia in flower, blooms the size of soup plates, seen from the top deck as a circle of pink and white splashes, and a man hunched and black with the sack of coal he was carrying on his back. Hazily green lime trees, about to come into leaf, cast shadows over a queue of people outside a cinema, plaiting the length of the street. Ellen thought of the tidy flat, that beautiful boy, and India Mayhew. India was two years younger than she was and had started at Hayfields halfway through the fourth year, when Ellen had been in the Sixth. She had been transparently defenceless, incautious and rash, one of those girls who stood out, who didn't know how to hammer herself into an acceptable form. She was always in trouble for one thing or another – lost gym shoes, talking in class. You'd see her talking to some sarcastic type, someone who liked making other girls' lives a misery, and she'd just offer herself up, fail to see it coming.

Ellen would hear them along a corridor, the usual suspects. What are you doing here, Africa, this wing's for seniors. Lost again? Shall I draw you a map? Your shoelaces are undone, America, and you haven't tied your tie properly. Blubbing again? Why don't you run home to Mummy? Oops, sorry, you haven't a mummy, have you?

Ellen sent them packing. After that, India had latched on to her. She hadn't meant to get caught up with India Mayhew, but sometimes you didn't choose someone, they chose you. And there had been nothing objectionable about India's behaviour, which had been, towards Ellen, impeccable. She was just *there*, trailing after her, sewn to her footsteps like a shadow, odd-looking back then, features too strong for her half-formed face, her uniform overlarge for her slender frame, enthusiastic when she should have been nonchalant, talking when she should have shut up. She had had a reputation for making up stories, embroidering the truth. Hayfields had been the sort of school where liars were ostracized, but Ellen could no more have slapped India down or told her to push off than she could have drowned an unwanted kitten.

And besides, behind the awkwardness and neediness there had been something in India that attracted. The world she alluded to – a brother, an aunt, a London life of fogs and concerts and coffee bars, had a certain rakish charm. And nothing was too much trouble for India. Ellen had never been sure whether you would call it loyalty or obstinacy. She wore you down: you let her post your letters or fetch your indoor shoes, even though you found it embarrassing.

India was fifteen when they first met, a difficult age to change school. I was expelled, India said, and Ellen, sensing confessions brimming, confidences approaching, hushed her. Some things were better not shared. Ungenerous of her, she now saw. She had been protecting herself, rejecting intimacy, when she might have helped India defuse a sense of failure and shame. Though Ellen had never been sure whether India was capable of feeling shame.

Shame wasn't something Ellen herself had had to tussle with, until the past sixteen months. She was used to acceptance, expected a certain amount of success. At first the shock of her dismissal from Gildersleve Hall had been mixed with disbelief and bewilderment. And humiliation, served up over and over again and with special panache whenever she happened to come across a former colleague or academic acquaintance. You're at Gildersleve Hall, aren't you? Then rebuttal, and explanations – there wasn't a painless way of telling people what had happened, for her or for them. She had become used to watching the expressions flicker through their eyes: surprise, then laboured tactfulness, pity or perhaps a touch of *Schadenfreude*. She found herself avoiding them, those work friends, those academic friends. Those Gildersleve friends, in particular. Once, catching sight of Martin Finch through the crowds at King's Cross station, she had hurried away down the platform, checking over her shoulder to make sure he hadn't seen her.

It had taken her six months to find another job. Staying with her parents in Wiltshire, the weather had never seemed more leadenly grey. She had read all the books she had always meant to read: *War and Peace* and *Anna Karenina* and *Crime and Punishment*, gloomy Russian novels which had suited her discouraged state of mind. After Dr Pharoah had sacked her, sometimes she had thought him bitterly unfair, but sometimes she had wondered whether she had been to blame. Whether she had reached her limit, whether he had seen something in her that had told him she would never be good enough. Never, ever.

Being academically successful had always been important to her. It had defined her. She would never forget the shock on her father's face when she told him that she had lost her job at Gildersleve Hall. Though shock had immediately been followed by sympathy and comfort, and though her family had loved her and reassured her and had offered her a space in which she could lick her wounds, she had minded very much. Retreat and regroup, her father advised her, but she had not at first known how. Nor had she realized how long it would take. The retreating was easy, it was the regrouping with which she had struggled: she could have papered her bedroom walls with the rejection letters. After a while, she had lowered her sights. A job growing cultures in a TB hospital, a lab assistant at a grammar school – anything would do. The glittering career she had once thought within her grasp – master's degree, research, maybe one day even a lectureship – slid away from her. She avoided risk, limited her ambitions. She had aimed too high, had not been good enough for Gildersleve Hall. She would not make that mistake twice.

She had become accustomed during her months in Cambridgeshire to being part of something exclusive, to being special. But she wasn't special any more, she was ordinary, and rather shabby with failure. When the letter had arrived from the hospital in St Pancras Way, offering her the position of junior lab assistant, she had felt, more than anything, relief, and had sent her letter of acceptance by return of post.

Ellen was nearing her stop. The woman beside her stood up too and Ellen offered to carry her shopping bags down the swaying spiral steps. The bus juddered to a halt and the conductor hauled a pushchair out on to the pavement. The younger child was slotted into the pushchair, the elder made to hold the handle, and bags were balanced.

Ellen walked up the main road then turned off down a side street. She had moved into the Islington lodging house at the end of June the previous year. It was a large, scruffy, rambling building, tenanted by her brother Joe and his friends, who were mostly students studying engineering and chemistry. There were several Daves, a couple of Steves, a Richard and a Mike. Their girlfriends were typists or nurses or they worked for a magazine or an advertising agency. None of them had heard of Gildersleve Hall, and none of them cared that Ellen Kingsley had once been sacked ignominiously.

Ellen was the only woman living there. She got on well enough with the Daves and Steves, as she tended to think of them. Sometimes she shared meals with them, sometimes they played poker into the night. Other times, when the humour was too juvenile or the shared kitchen too messy, she retreated to her room. It was small and narrow, on the north side of the house so rather dark, but she had furnished it herself, unlike the rooms in hall of her college days or Mrs Bryant's bungalow in Copfield. Her first real room of her own. Her parents had sent up a bed and chest of drawers from home but Ellen had bought everything else in London – a desk and chair from a junk shop, a rug from an inexpensive local store, curtains and bedspread that she had made herself. Her books and a few ornaments filled the shelves, and her dresses hung on a rail. For the first time she was living with her own taste rather than someone else's.

Here, she read books and wrote letters or mended clothes and listened to the radio. In this way, she heard of the great things that happened in 1953: the coronation of Elizabeth II, the conquest of Everest, the revelation of the double helix structure of DNA. Now and then she had the feeling that the world was going on without her, exciting and novel, while she lay on the bed reading Turgenev or listening to *Friday Night Is Music Night*.

Reaching the house, Ellen unlocked the front door and went inside. As she climbed the stairs, she noticed that the bathroom was empty, so she dashed to her room, gathered up her towel and sponge bag, ran back down a floor and bolted the bathroom door behind her. While she was soaking in the hot water, Joe tapped on the door to ask her whether she was having supper. Ellen said no, she might go to a concert. Then: what had she done today? Nothing much, she said, swooshing water with the flat palm of her hand so that it sloshed against the side of the bath. I met an old friend. And thought, was that what India was? Or did you just, after a while, find it easier to fall into India's way of thinking?

India met Garrett in Dean Street. She was wearing her silk dress, which was the intense, inarguable blue of morning glories. The dress had come from a shop in Bond Street. Ed, who worked in the City and was in his mid-thirties, plump, balding and unhappily married, had bought it for her. He had come round to the shop one day after work with a box, the dress wrapped in tissue paper inside it, tucked under his arm. 'You don't mind, do you?' he said, when he gave it to her. 'It's just that I saw it in the window and it's the same colour as your eyes.' He had gone pink as he had said it, so, to reassure him that she wasn't

128

assuming that he was assuming anything, she had kissed him.

Just now, India was short of cash. She was only a very junior assistant in the art supply shop and Sebastian's gardening jobs brought in even less money. Neither of them spent much but they seemed to lurch between just about managing and slipping into debt. This month, no matter how she jiggled the bills and no matter how hard she thought we don't need this or that, there wasn't enough to pay both the electricity and the phone. India supposed that theoretically they could have done without the telephone but she would have hated that. And she had to pay back Ellen. She didn't want Ellen to think her the sort of person who didn't repay debts.

Ed would have lent her money, but she didn't like to borrow from Ed. India had her principles: she borrowed only from people she wouldn't feel bad about if she failed to repay. She had accepted the gift of the frock because it would have made Ed miserable if she had refused it, but money was different. And anyway, Ed was away, on holiday with his adulterous wife.

The French pub smelled of red wine and cigarettes. The small barroom was as dark as night, packed to the gunwales with drinkers. Absinthe and pastis were sold at the bar, as well as wine and beer. Some of the notices on the walls were in French, a legacy from the war, when Free French soldiers used to drink here. India, who had never been abroad, even so caught the drift of the alien, the exile.

India and Garrett squeezed into a corner with their friends. You had to shout to be heard over the noise. Vinnie Spencer, who was a saxophonist in Garrett's band, had brought along a girl called Justine. Justine's hair was cut in a choppy bob and she was wearing black slacks and a baggy black jumper. She told India about her job, dancing in a revue. 'It's pretty awful, really. I play a cat, with ears and whiskers, but it'll pay the rent until my poems are published.'

'When are they being published?'

'I don't know, I haven't sent them off yet. I've been trying to think of a title. I can't decide between *The Yellow Moon* and *Rain in the Afternoon*. What do you think?'

'*Rain in the Afternoon*,' said India, very definitely. 'You couldn't lend me a couple of quid, could you?'

''Fraid not.' Justine flicked ash on the floor. 'Pretending to be a cat doesn't pay *that* well.'

India and Garrett headed off to the Colony Room, which was above a trattoria along Dean Street. A wall of people seethed round the bamboo-clad bar, which was presided over by Muriel Belcher. Muriel had a long oval face, dark hair swept smoothly back from her high forehead, sharp black eyes and a nose which curved like the beak of a hawk.

Oliver, who owned the garage that did up the cars that Garrett delivered, was slumped in a corner at one end of the bar. If he was flush, he might lend her some cash, India thought hopefully. He was holding his head in his hands, but whenever his eyelids drooped shut an elbow would slip off the bar, jerking him awake. Garrett said hello and Oliver mumbled something back. 'Pissed as a lord,' said Muriel Belcher crossly. 'You can take him away if he causes trouble.' India mentally crossed Oliver off her list.

Vinnie caught up with them; someone had told him that Peachey was giving a party so they all meandered off to Tite Street. The door to Peachey's house was opened by a young man with curly red hair. He eyed India and her friends, drew on a small black cigarette, then exhaled smoke.

'Oh, you can come in, I suppose.'

'Hello, Simon,' said India. 'Is Laurence here?'

'Didn't you know? He's in hospital. Caught measles and nearly died.' Simon snorted. 'Rather undignified, I call it, catching measles at his age.'

Inside the house, the lights were low and Billie Holliday's voice permeated the rooms, which smelled of the heavy oriental perfume Peachey wore, underpinned by a stale mustiness. The dark purple walls of the hallway were decorated by a mirror with a gilt frame and a large painting of a nude, a big-nosed, black-eyed, salmon-pink woman, reclining on a purple couch. A chipped marble nymph stood at the bottom of the stairs, one of her arms upstretched, as if she was reaching up to change a lightbulb. Garrett hung his scarf on the statue's raised hand.

India went downstairs to the kitchen. Peachey's kitchen smelled even worse than the rest of the house. The sink overflowed with dirty crockery and cats were feeding from saucers scattered over the floor. A big white Persian cat, a giant ball of fluff sporting what India could only think of as moustaches, trod fastidiously over the debris on the draining board.

Mrs Peachey herself was sitting at the kitchen table, smoking, a tabby cat on her lap. Peachey was tall and broad-shouldered and her long, elegant face had the creased and crumpled sexlessness of old age. She was wearing a dark green satin dress, of a waistless style out of fashion since the 1920s. The cat stirred and she ran a gnarled and wrinkled hand along its back.

Spying India, Peachey glared at her. 'I'm out of gin. Those bastards have drunk it all. It's ridiculous, so early in the evening. You don't happen to have any on you, do you?'

'I'm afraid not. I was going to ask you if you could lend me a fiver.'

'Haven't a bean, darling. That's the trouble with getting old, you never have any money. If I was twenty, I'd model for John or Sickert and I'd be flush again.' Peachey added snidely, 'Hot little piece like you needn't be short of cash. You should ask Bernie, he's got a few bob.'

'Is he here?'

'No, I won't have him in my house after the last time. You want to be careful, India. He might fall for someone else.' Peachey gave a cackle of laughter and the tabby cat bristled. 'Where's that beautiful boy of yours?'

'Garrett? He's upstairs.'

'Tell him to come down here and say hello to me.'

India went back upstairs. In the sitting room, which was painted a deep strawberry pink, couples were dancing. There were other paintings on the walls, mostly nudes, of Peachey in her heyday. India had tried modelling once, but had found it tiresome and impossible, all that sitting still.

Someone put on another record. Justine began to dance, by herself at first, her long, black-clad limbs making sinuous movements, and then Simon joined her.

Vinnie said, 'How are you, India?'

'I'm very well, thank you. Peachey won't lend me any money.'

'You must have caught her in a mood, the sour old cow.' Vinnie gave her a sympathetic glance. 'I could let you have something at the end of the week.'

India wasn't sure whether they would still have a phone by the end of the week. 'Sweet of you,' she said, and squeezed his hand. Then Garrett pulled her into the centre of the room, and she tucked herself into his arms and closed her eyes, pressing her cheek against his as they danced.

Shortly afterwards, Peachey, still in a temper, threw them all out of the house. India was feeling hungry, so Garrett bought fish and chips, which they shared. Then they argued about whether to go to Bernie's party. Eventually India caved in and said all right, for an hour, so they caught an Underground train to Mayfair.

The nightclub was the sort of place that instantly made India feel happy. The glitter of light on chandelier and champagne glass and the rhythm of the band made her spirits fizz. Bernie and a dozen of his friends – men in sharp suits and girls in expensive frocks – were sitting round a large circular table.

Bernie was only a couple of inches taller than India herself, and had a stout, barrel-shaped torso and short little legs. His face was smooth and oval and brown, like a nut, and his voice was pitched high for a man of his rotundity. When she had first heard him speak India had wanted to laugh.

Bernie took his cigar out of his mouth and gave India a nod. 'Hello, gorgeous.'

'Hello, Bernie. Happy birthday.'

As she kissed his cheek he patted her bottom. 'Someone get the girl champagne,' he called, and a glass was handed to her.

'Sit down, India,' said Bernie, and the man sitting next to him stood up.

'No, I want to dance.'

Bernie gave her a look. 'Frank'll keep the seat warm for you, then,' and some of his friends laughed. 'Skittish, are we?'

'You know me, Bernie darling, I don't like sitting still.' She gave him a big smile and left the table.

There were a lot of other people she knew at the club and when she wasn't dancing, she went from table to table, talking to people. Now and then she glanced over to Bernie's party. She had the feeling that he was watching her. India had once seen a pike at an aquarium. It had had eyes like Bernie's: unblinking, dead-looking.

Garrett had met Bernie through his friend, Clive, who let out the flats. Bernie owned flats and houses throughout London, which he sublet to people like Clive, who had to hand on to him the rent, minus their cut, whether the properties had tenants or not. Clive wanted to keep in with Bernie and Garrett wanted to keep in with Clive. Garrett also enjoyed the spill-off from Bernie's fortune that occasionally reached their rocky little shore – and so did she, if she was honest. Who wouldn't enjoy a party in the Blue Duck nightclub where all the drinks were paid for, or a dinner in a West End restaurant? But she had learned long ago that there was always a price to pay, and there was something about the way Bernie looked at her that gave her the creeps. But then, the bills. Apart from the utter dreariness of the phone or the electricity being cut off, Sebastian would be alarmed. Sebastian liked life to tick along in a predictable way and he would start imagining awful things, like them losing the flat. So, Bernie. It frightened her. But, Vinnie, Oliver, Laurence, Peachey – she was running out of options.

One of Bernie's friends tapped her on the shoulder and told her they were cutting the cake. Bernie's cake was rather more splendid than the cake India had baked for Sebastian's birthday, with squirls of royal icing and thirty-five red candles, all matching. A waiter lit the candles with a flourish and Bernie blew them out with a sharp little puff.

He patted the seat beside him. 'You need to eat your cake, India.'

Reluctantly, she sat down. 'Where's Garrett?' she asked.

'I sent him on an errand. Girl like you shouldn't be wasting her time on someone like Garrett Parker.'

India cursed Garrett under her breath.

The cake was cut, Bernie's thigh pressed against hers. 'Do you like to play blackjack, India?' asked Bernie.

'I don't know.'

'Time to find out, then. Some of us are going on to one of my places.'

She unpeeled the icing from the cake. 'Card games are so boring.'

'Not if you're playing them for money, they're not.' Bernie popped a piece of cake into his mouth. 'The house always wins, of course. But if you own the house . . .' He winked.

She could feel her resolve weakening. She imagined going to the casino with Bernie and winning lots of money, paying all the bills, paying Ellen back, buying some new clothes, perhaps. But then, out of the corner of her eye, she caught a glimpse of Michael Colebrook in the crowd, and she stood up, saying, 'Sorry, Bernie, not tonight. Another time, perhaps,' then squeezed out from the table, crossed the dance floor and tapped Michael on the shoulder.

Michael turned and smiled at her. 'Hello, India. Would you like to dance?'

Michael Colebrook lived in Half Moon Street and worked for the Foreign Office. He had bright brown eyes like a robin's topped with short, thick black brows. India had met him more than a year ago, when she and her then boyfriend had had a big argument and she had stormed off, realizing too late that she had no money in her purse. They had quarrelled in Southwark, which had meant a long walk back to the flat. She had been wearing high heels and had taken them off to walk home. Michael had stopped his car as she was crossing Waterloo Bridge, and had offered her a lift. She had accepted, because she had blisters, and he had proved to be the nicest man, not a rapist or murderer at all, and had driven her home. Since then their friendship had flourished.

She said, 'Actually, darling, if you don't mind, I'd like to leave.'

Michael fetched her coat from the cloakroom and they left the club. In the taxi, India said, 'You couldn't lend me some money, could you, Michael?'

'Of course, how much do you need?'

'Ten pounds, I'm afraid. It might be for a while.'

'A birthday present.'

'It's not my birthday.'

'An early birthday present, then.' He took two ten-pound notes out of his wallet and handed them to her.

'You're very sweet.' She tucked the money into her purse. 'I should probably marry you.'

'No, you shouldn't. I would bore you within an

afternoon.' The taxi's windscreen wipers thwacked at the rain and she rested her head on his shoulder.

The laboratory was in an oblong, single-storey brick building at the back of the hospital. Through the windows came the rattle of trolleys of dirty linen and the conversation of the porters, who liked to smoke in the asphalt area between the lab and the laundry.

The laboratory's work was overseen by Professor Malik. Working for Professor Malik was very different from working for Dr Pharoah. There wasn't the competition, the jostling for position. Malik was Anglo-Indian, thin, sixtyish, never raised his voice and was calmly encouraging no matter how much work there was to be got through, even if the consultants were breathing down his neck, impatient for results. He was unfailingly civil to his staff and treated the female employees with exactly the same courtesy as the men. Ellen liked Professor Malik and almost trusted him. Almost. She seemed to have lost the capacity for absolute trust.

The samples of blood and tissue would come in from the wards several times a day, and then there would the rush to analyse them and prepare cultures and slides. Ellen's job was to label the samples, every test tube and dish, and to copy the labels on to a check sheet. Hundreds of samples a day, each one to be labelled clearly and accurately, no room for slip-ups or poor handwriting because lives depended on speed and precision. In any spare moments between the trolleys arriving, she cleaned glassware. Again, no room for error or cross-contamination. If there was a rush in the early evening she stayed on, working overtime as the victims of car crashes or patients with high fevers were taken on to the wards. She didn't mind staying late; there was a camaraderie about the lab, a sense of working closely with each other in the quiet evenings that reminded her of Gildersleve at its best.

One evening, it was almost eight o'clock by the time she got home to the lodging house. From the corridor, she heard voices from the kitchen. India's: *You have to wait until you can smell the gas or it won't light.* And Joe's: *Sounds lethal. I'll come round and have a look, if you like.*

Ellen felt tired; she wanted to kick off her shoes, peel off her stockings, lie in a hot bath, and instead, here was India Mayhew, her new best friend, in *her* house.

She went into the kitchen. Joe was standing at the sink and India was sitting at the table. A handful of Daves and Steves were in the kitchen as well, opening cans of beans and scraping the burnt bits from toast.

Joe said, 'Hi, Ellen,' and India did her smile, and all the toast-scrapers and can-openers stopped what they were doing and admired her.

'Hello, Joe. Hello, everyone. Hello, India.'

'How lovely to see you, Ellen. Joe's been looking after me so well.'

'Only a cup of coffee,' said Joe, who was washing up.

'But a simply gorgeous cup of coffee.' That smile again.

India opened a large white woven-leather handbag and delved through handkerchieves, lipsticks and scribbled scraps of paper. She found a purse and offered some coins to Ellen. 'Five shillings and sixpence. Thank you so much.'

'Did Sebastian like the books?'

'Enormously.'

Joe said to Ellen, 'There's some corned beef, if you want it.'

'I'm fine, thanks, I had a sandwich at the hospital.'

'Good day?'

'Long.' Ellen sat down and slid her feet out of her shoes.

'I brought you this,' said India, and, with the air of a magician taking a rabbit from a hat, produced a bottle of wine from her bag. 'It's to say thank you for helping me with, well, the bookshop. And to celebrate us meeting up again, of course.'

The wine was a 1938 Petrus. Ellen wondered how India could afford such a bottle – slipped beneath her coat, perhaps, in some dusty Soho wine merchants?

'It's kind of you, India, but there was no need.'

'A friend of mine gave it to Sebastian for his birthday, but he doesn't like wine. I thought you might like it.'

Ellen felt ashamed of herself. There was she, judging India, and yet how she hated others to judge her. Guilt, and the desire for a drink, made her say, 'Let's open it, then.'

Glasses were found, wine was poured. Someone began to fry eggs while India wandered around, opening cupboards and leafing through the books on the table and chatting to people and saying things like, 'What a sweet little vase,' and, 'You're all so brainy.' And time passed and one of the Daves went out to buy beer and crisps and Ellen could not afterwards put her finger on when or how it happened, that alteration in chemistry, that addition of a catalyst that so lifted the mood of the evening that she forgot her tiredness and didn't bother to worry about the queue for the bathroom and enjoyed herself more than she had for months.

In the kitchen of the house in Tufnell Park, every surface was covered with mixing bowls and saucepans, and more pans were simmering on the hob. The radio was turned up loud, something about Princess Margaret. Coming home from work, Riley started to wash up the dishes in the sink, but Pearl said, 'Don't do that. Sit down, I'm cooking you a special meal.'

'Are we celebrating something?'

'Does there need to be a reason for me to cook you a nice dinner?' She was staring at him, her eyes big, a whisk in one hand.

'Of course not.'

'I couldn't remember when I last made you a proper meal. Was it yesterday?'

It seemed longer, but he said, 'Yes, I think so. What are you cooking?'

'Prawn cocktail – no, no,' she flicked through a recipe book, 'shrimp and orange cocktail.'

'Sounds lovely.'

'And beef pie and lemon pudding. I bought some wine.'

A bottle of red was nestling on the windowsill among the pan scourers and washing-up liquid. Pearl topped up her own glass, looked round, found a tumbler on the draining board, and poured wine into it. Crimson splashes trailed down the sink.

'What was I doing?' she said. 'Oh, yes, the egg whites.' She tucked a bowl under her arm to whisk the egg whites. A minute's beating and then she put the bowl down and poked something bobbing in a saucepan. Then she peered into the oven, and, scooping back her hair from her forehead, said, puzzled, 'I was in the middle of something, wasn't I?'

'The egg whites. Can I do anything?'

'I *can* cook, you know,' she said, giving him a cold look. 'Honestly, John, sometimes I think you think I'm completely useless.' Then her expression lightened. 'Go and find some candles. We must have candles, I *adore* candles. They'll make the house less dreary.'

Riley went upstairs to look in on Annie, who was sleeping, and then to the bedroom, where he hung up his jacket and loosened his tie. Then he glanced through the day's post and unearthed the candles from the cupboard beneath the stairs. And all the time he did these things, something uneasy and cold uncoiled in his stomach.

He heard a crash and a scream and hurried back to the kitchen.

'Pearl? What's the matter?'

She was standing by the cooker, holding a saucepan, staring into it. 'The potatoes have boiled dry!' She slammed the saucepan on the hob. 'Look at them! Ruined! All that work! Why didn't you tell me? You must have smelled them! Why do I have to do everything?'

'It's OK, I'll sort it out.' He reached to take the saucepan but she snatched it from him, crashing it down on the hob once more, her teeth bared.

There was a cry from upstairs. Pearl hissed, 'Now look, she's woken up! It's all your fault!'

Riley walked out of the room. He realized as he went upstairs that his jaw was aching from tension.

Annie was sitting up in bed, her fists clenched. 'Daddy, I heard a noise,' she whispered.

'It's all right, sweetheart. Mummy dropped something, that's all.' He stroked her hair. 'Go back to sleep.'

Annie lay back on the pillow. While he waited for her to go back to sleep, Riley listened, alert for sounds from the lower floor of the house. It seemed to him that the only thing he and Pearl now had in common was their love of their daughter. He had learned to judge Pearl's mood from the way she looked at him, the tone of her voice and the fast see-saw of her temper. He had taught himself to detect melancholy, anger and jealousy at a glance. Tonight's was a mood he was familiar with: the frantic activity and enthusiasm, interspersed with bouts of anger and suspicion. Challenge her and she'd either dissolve into tears or hurl herself at him, screaming, beating her fists against his chest.

So he appeased her, for Annie's sake, because he did not want his daughter to grow up in a battleground. And yet he was finding it harder and harder to act out this travesty of affection, or to shake off, even temporarily, the suffocating sensation of being trapped. He could see no way out of the situation, either for himself or for Pearl. Marriage was binding, a promise made to be kept for life, in sickness and in health, until death parted them. Annie needed a father and a mother. Sometimes Pearl still claimed to need him, to love him. On his part, all that remained of the passion he had once felt for her were a few cold curlings of pity.

Annie had fallen asleep again; Riley went back down to the kitchen. Pearl was sitting at the table, her head in her hands. She looked up as he came in. 'Sorry,' she whispered. 'I'm sorry, John. I shouldn't have shouted at you.'

'It doesn't matter. You're trying to do too much, that's all.'

'I *can* do it.' Her voice quavered.

'Of course you can. Just, a bit at a time, perhaps.'

'I'm so tired. If only I could sleep . . .' She looked up at him, her eyes swimming with tears. 'You do still love me, don't you? I wouldn't blame you if you didn't, but you do, don't you?'

He put a hand on her shoulder. Her body quivered like a taut string and she leaned her head against his arm. But he couldn't find the words she wanted him to say; ashes seemed to sear his tongue, and his hand moved mechanically as he stroked her hair.

The Mayhews' flat became a refuge for Ellen from the studenty grubbiness of the Islington lodging house. India and Sebastian had inherited it from their Aunt Rachel, who had been their mother's elder sister. India showed Ellen a photograph of Rachel. A pleasant, serious face, framed by a serious wartime hairstyle, looked back at Ellen from the black and white portrait.

When Ellen asked India about her parents, India said, 'My father was killed in the Blitz. My mother died a year and a half later. She was a dancer, quite a famous one. She danced at Sadler's Wells.' Then she changed the subject.

Once a week or so, India invited Ellen to tea. Suppers with the Mayhews were unorthodox: oxtail soup followed by slices of orange, or chips, cooked in a frying pan and sprinkled with salt and vinegar, and then powdery meringues from a baker's. India always cooked and Sebastian always cleared up. Ellen found it impossible to imagine the other way round. India dropped floured fillets of plaice into a pan and fat sizzled. A cigarette in one hand, a wooden spoon in the other as she stirred a cheese sauce. Peeling potatoes, she wore a striped apron over a dress of blue silk.

Sebastian dabbed a cloth at the flour on the draining board and mopped the floor. Ellen always offered to wash up after supper and Sebastian always politely refused. If the phone rang, it was always India who answered it. If, as happened very occasionally, the call was for Sebastian, he approached it cautiously, holding the receiver a careful distance from his ear before saying hello. India always opened the door of the flat to let Ellen in, never Sebastian, as if he couldn't quite be sure what was waiting outside. Sebastian rarely started up a conversation, but sometimes, when the three of them were sitting at the table having supper, he would thread his hands together, pressing them outwards, bob his head and then look up, smiling that same sweet smile Ellen had noticed the first time she had met him, and proceed to tell a story about his day.

India liked to go shopping in Oxford Street. Inside Selfridges, she fingered fabric, testing its weight, shaking her head over the cut and finish of a blouse. Then she would slip her feet into a pair of high heels and walk up and down. Ellen felt a certain tension, shopping with India. She found herself keeping an eye on her as she came out of the changing rooms, measuring the fatness of her handbag and the bulk beneath her coat.

The summer dresses came in, full-skirted, tight-bodiced cottons and linens. The frock Ellen bought was coral-coloured, cap-sleeved and narrow at the waist, tied with a bow. *Yes*, said India, with an approving nod as Ellen came out of the changing room. All her savings, she thought, on one glorious frock, and all because India Mayhew had somehow slipped herself back into her life.

Sometimes India's boyfriend, Garrett Parker, came to tea. Garrett was dark and handsome, with flashing eyes and a beguiling grin. Inside the Mayhews' kitchen, he taught Ellen a new dance step. He put his palms on her shoulders and looked into her eyes, swaying his hips and moving in close, a smile playing around the corners of his mouth. Over the top of his head, Ellen saw India, sitting on the draining board, a hand pressed against her mouth, laughing.

Then India and Garrett demonstrated the dance step. Garrett was wearing paint-stained overalls and India had on a faded cotton dress. They kept catching each other's eyes and guffawing, but sometimes the laughter died and was replaced by heat. It felt intrusive, watching them.

Ellen turned her back and looked out of the kitchen window. Sap-green leaves were unfurling on a horse chestnut in a neighbour's garden and cars were queuing outside the garage over the road. The gramophone scratched out a tune and the room smelled steamy and stale, of cooking. No one had ever looked at her like that. Had she ever looked at a man with such longing in her eyes? She remembered gazing out of the window of her lab at Gildersleve Hall, to where Alec Hunter had walked through the copse: the catch in her throat, the tug of something she thirsted for, out of her reach. More than a year and a half ago, she had fallen in love with Alec Hunter. She wondered where he was now. On his island, she supposed, with Andrée, and into her mind came a picture of the two of them walking hand in hand along a shore pounded by winter storms.

She had not forgotten him, though she had tried. She only minded that she had not completely stopped minding.

Riley woke in the night. Switching on the light, he saw that Pearl's side of the bed was empty. When she couldn't sleep, she sometimes went into the spare room. He got up, put on the bedside light and pulled on a pair of trousers, then looked in the spare room, bathroom and Annie's room. No Pearl.

He glanced at his watch. It was ten past three in the morning and, as he walked downstairs, he felt the grey lifelessness of the house during this, the dead centre of the night. Pearl wasn't in the living room, dining room or kitchen. Out of the kitchen window, he caught a flicker of movement, a gleam of scarlet fabric and the orange tip of a cigarette.

He went outside. It was May, still cold. Pearl was wearing her red silk kimono and was walking up and down the garden.

He said, 'Pearl, what are you doing?'

She kept on walking. 'I was thinking,' she said, 'what if we went to live in Cornwall? We could go to the beach every day. Annie would adore it. It would be so *lovely*!'

'Come back into the house.'

'No, listen to me, John, I want to live in Cornwall!'

'No,' he said sharply. 'It's out of the question.' He took her elbow but she shook him off, and, staring at him, gave a furious hiss.

'I hate it here! I hate this horrible bloody house!'

He found himself examining her coolly, almost as if she was a suspect he was interviewing, scrutinizing her features, which were contorted with anger, and her hair, which fell in wild snaky locks around her face, before moving to the red kimono, which flapped loosely around her thin night-dress, and her bare, grass-stained feet.

'We're staying in this house,' he said. 'We're not going to move again, Pearl, so you'd better start trying to make the best of this place. If there's anything else you wish to say to me then please come indoors and we can talk there.'

She gave him an icy glare, then looked away. 'There's nothing I want to say to you, John. Nothing at all.'

Bernie was waiting outside the shop when India left for her lunch break. He offered to take her to Wheeler's and she said no thanks, she only had an hour for lunch. Doesn't matter, he said, they could do it there and back in an hour, easy. And she had shopping to do. Lee would do it; Bernie smacked his chauffeur on the back of his head. Lee liked shopping, didn't he? Lee said, 'Yes, boss.' Lee's hair, a light ginger, was cropped close, and his skin was pale, allowing India to see the flush which travelled up the back of his neck to the top of his scalp.

It seemed easier for India to say yes, too, so she climbed into the car and Lee drove them to Old Compton Street. Then she had to invent errands for Lee – soap and sugar, keep it simple or he might take hours. At a table by the front window, India and Bernie ate fish and potatoes and salad. Bernie talked about himself, mostly. It was easy enough to get Bernie to talk about himself, and she thought she had got away with it and was about to remind Bernie that she needed to go back to the shop, when he said, 'You think you're a smart little miss, don't you, India?'

She made herself meet his eyes. 'Not particularly.'

'Buy you dinner, take you to nice places.' Bernie dabbed his mouth with his napkin and inspected his fingernails. He was always fastidiously clean. 'And what do I get back?'

'I haven't asked you for anything. You asked me to lunch,' she reminded him.

'Oh yes, I did.' Bernie buffed a nail on his napkin.

'I have to go back to the shop now or I'll be late.'

'Like your job, do you, India?'

'Yes, very much.'

'I could find you a job in one of my casinos. All you'd have to do is to wear a nice frock and smile at people. You wouldn't have to get up early or nothing.'

'I'm happy where I am, thanks.'

'Can't pay much.' He took a note out of his wallet and put it on the table. 'How do you manage, you and your brother?'

India stiffened. She had never told Bernie about Sebastian. How did he know? 'You mustn't worry about me, Bernie,' she said lightly. 'I'm not short of cash. My aunt left me lots of money. I've loads of it stashed away in a bank.'

'Oh, I don't think so,' Bernie said. His eyes, the

150

brown-grey of mud at the bottom of a pond, surveyed her. 'I really don't think so.'

Lee drove her back to the shop and handed her the carrier bag with the shopping in it. As well as sugar and soap, there was a box of Black Magic and half a dozen packets of nylons, the sight of which made India growl like a dog. She was ten minutes late back from her lunch break and Miss Maloney told her off. Throughout the afternoon she kept doing things wrong – getting the change muddled and dropping all the watercolour brushes out of their wooden box and having to sort them back into their compartments. She was rattled and she couldn't concentrate and that was the truth of it. Bernie had rattled her. On her way home from work she gave the carrier bag of stuff that Lee had bought to an old woman who was sitting in an alleyway, begging for change. She felt some regret for the nylons, but she had her principles.

Coming into the flat, she noticed a bunch of bluebells in a vase on the centre of the table. Sebastian must have picked them from one of his gardens. The stems looked bruised and the flowers were drooping. India would have liked to chuck them away, too. She hated bluebells. How had Bernie found out about Sebastian? Had Garrett said something? Garrett had a big mouth. Had Bernie meant anything by mentioning Sebastian, or had it just been a passing comment? India was afraid that everything Bernie said meant something.

She ran a bath, undressed, and lay in the soapy water,

feeling the grime of the day float away. She wondered whether she should go to bed with Bernie, get it over and done with, and then perhaps he would leave her alone. But she recoiled from the thought of those fish eyes looking at her, those soft little hands touching her. And what if he didn't leave her alone afterwards, what if he expected to keep her in his collection, one of those silly, simpering women who went to clubs and parties with him?

The trouble was that she had got in too deep. *Buy you dinner, take you to nice places.* This was true. She had never before today dined with Bernie alone, Garrett and Clive had always been there as well. But she had known that Bernie was after her. She wasn't stupid, like Garrett, who didn't notice such things. Garrett thought Bernie was going to offer him 'business', as he put it, because Garrett lived in a world where things always worked out for the best. India had gone along with it partly to keep Garrett happy and partly because she enjoyed the glamour. The Mayfair clubs and the dinners in restaurants in Piccadilly and St James, brushing shoulders with the rich and the famous – if a rather tarnished rich and famous – had made her feel good. Had made her feel *safe*. This was all she wanted, to feel safe, her and Sebastian, because she could not feel safe if Sebastian was not safe. And Bernie's remark had unnerved her.

India climbed out of the bath and wrapped a towel round herself. She couldn't be bothered putting in rollers, and the steam had curled her hair so that it rippled away from her face. She made a cup of tea and some toast and then sat down on the sofa.

Her gaze was caught once more by the bluebells. There had been bluebells at the house in the woods when they had first gone to live there. That had been the year after her father had died. He had been killed in the London Blitz, in 1940, when India was eight and Sebastian four. He had been on leave from the army and a bomb had hit the bus on which he was travelling. Rachel had told India this afterwards, when she had been trying to sort it all out in her head.

The house in the woods was the first house that India could truly remember. She knew they had lived in other houses beforehand, but could only remember pieces of them – a basement courtyard, a bathroom papered with pale green fish. The house was surrounded on three sides by woodland, acres of it, a forest, really. No neighbours for miles. A narrow country road ran along the front of the house. Whenever a vehicle passed, she and Sebastian ran to the front gate to have a look.

Their water came from a well in the garden. Water was supposed to come out of taps; they had all been dismayed by the well. 'Like in a fairy story,' their mother said to them the day they moved in, trying to make the best of it. India had a clear memory of her mother, wearing a cotton summer dress printed with flowers, a cigarette in her mouth, hauling the arm of the pump up and down. Her mother had been called Cindy and she had been a dancer before she married

Daddy. She had had long flaxen hair which she rolled up in a sort of sausage all round her head. She had been very thin and her joints had hurt from too much dancing. 'My poor bones,' her mother often said.

India had taken over the getting of water. She hadn't minded: the crunch and press of the pump, the water squirting into the metal bucket were satisfying. When her mother's friends called, they took over the task. Men in army khaki or navy or air force blue nonchalantly operated the pump one-handed. It was fun that first summer. They had picnics in the garden and parties in the house when Cindy's friends came to stay. Another memory: her mother with a green satin flower in her hair, a cigarette in one hand and a glass of sherry in the other, laughing and dancing. Then the men went away and fetching the water was India's job again.

Going to the shops was also India's job. Cindy wrote her a list, frowning, pencil in hand, and India took Cindy's purse and a shopping bag. Sometimes she took Sebastian with her. India had a bicycle and Sebastian a tricycle, found for them who-knows-where in that austere wartime Britain by one of Cindy's friends, Neil, a naval officer. India's bike was too large for her and she had to stand on the pedals, and Sebastian was terribly slow on his tricycle, but it had a little basket on the back where they could put things. The shop was a long way away, on the main road, past the church and the school that India and Sebastian went to. It sold everything: pencils and handkerchieves and knitting wool, as well as food, though you could never be sure what exactly it would sell on any particular day.

Once, not long after they came to live in the house in the woods, the three of them walked to the shop on a fine summer's afternoon. Cindy put on a nice frock and let India wear her party dress (lilac net) and a straw hat. Sebastian wore his pale blue shorts and shirt. It was an uphill walk to the shop and they had to stop several times for Cindy to rest. When they reached the shop, they discovered that Mrs Day was out of writing paper. 'It's the war, dear,' she said to Cindy. 'I could let you have a couple of postcards.' Mrs Day, who was enormously fat and wore a flowered pinny over a mud-coloured dress, and whose stockings (also mud-coloured) were rolled down to her ankles, admired India's frock and said what a pretty little girl she was and gave her and Sebastian an apple. Cindy bought the postcards and they walked back down the hill. After they got back to the house, Cindy lay down on the sofa and India made tea for herself and Sebastian and put Sebastian to bed.

In the winter, her mother's friends visited less often. Mummy looked sad, so India tried to cheer her up by making her cups of tea and putting on the gramophone. They sang along to 'My Funny Valentine', and her mother taught India how to do the quickstep, just a few steps at a time, because of her bones. The house was cold, and often Sebastian climbed into India's bed at night, to keep warm. India told him stories about an imaginary land of hills and lakes and castles. When India described to Sebastian their voyage in a sailing boat, she heard the soft beat of the breeze in the sail and trailed her hand in cool crystal water.

At Christmas, the naval officer, Neil, came to stay. India listened to them arguing behind the closed door of the bedroom. 'It won't do, Lucinda,' she heard Neil say loudly. 'You have to think of those children.' The next day, Neil had gone and her mother took to her bed again.

Snow fell in January, marooning them in a fairy-tale forest. India and Sebastian put on their boots and coats and ran outside. India's boots were too small for her and pinched. The snowdrifts were taller than Sebastian and clods of snow slid with a satisfying *flump* from the branches to the ground. Because of the snow, India walked up the hill rather than take the bike. At the shop, Mrs Day said to her, 'And how's that mother of yours?' and India said politely, 'She's very well, thank you.'

But she wasn't. Mummy spent whole days resting in bed. Sometimes India heard her crying. When India asked her what was wrong, she said she missed Daddy. In the evenings, she liked India to rub her feet, which were as cold as ice. India filled hot-water bottles for her, boiling up a kettle on the stove. One day, after the snow thawed, Mummy wrote a number on a piece of paper and told India to go to the call box and phone the doctor. The telephone kiosk was on the main road, near the shop, so India cycled. The doctor came later that day and left a bottle of pills. The pills made her mother sleep, and after that things were better.

India was missing more and more school, what with looking after the house and Sebastian and her mother when she was unwell. It was a horrible school anyway, with hardly any books and a lot of going to church. The other boys and girls, tough country children with sensible, ordinary names like Mary and Joan or Bill and Peter, teased India and Sebastian for their odd names and the way they spoke. Sebastian hated school and cried the mornings she made him go; he had learned to read anyway, and if he was happier with their mother and playing in the garden, then why not let him stay at home instead of dragging him weeping up the hill?

India kept hoping that Neil would come back, but he didn't. Often, weeks went by without them seeing anyone other than Mrs Day at the shop. The house was starting to look dirty and Sebastian was growing out of all his clothes. Now and then, Cindy would have a go at the washing, carrying all the linen downstairs, putting it in to soak and hauling it through the mangle, but then she would wander off to read a book or sit in the porch and have a smoke. Sometimes a day later India would come across a basket of washing in the scullery or abandoned in the garden, still damp and oddly smelly. 'Oh dear, I wish I was a better housekeeper,' Cindy would say, picking up one of Sebastian's vests and sniffing it.

India knew that if her mother wasn't much of a

housekeeper then neither was she. She tried, but it was hard to think of things for lunch and tea, what with there being so little in the shops. She had a look in Cindy's recipe book, which told her how to make things called Steak Diane and Sole Meunière, but Mrs Day's shop didn't sell steak or sole. Cindy wrote on the shopping list 'luncheon meat' or 'tin of peas' but sometimes there weren't any of those in Mrs Day's shop either.

Mrs Day tried to teach India how to use their ration points wisely, but Mrs Day also said things like, 'Your mother can use that to make a nice stew with some mutton from the butcher,' or, 'Tell your mother to put the cabbage in a fish pie.' From this, India guessed that Mrs Day assumed that her mother did the bulk of her shopping in Andover, the nearest town. She didn't tell Mrs Day that her mother hadn't been to Andover since Christmas, and so hadn't visited a butcher or a fishmonger, because that seemed a failing, something that marked them out as deficient, not quite right. India had begun to be afraid that someone, some figure of authority, perhaps a teacher or a policeman, might decide to do something about them. So she just said, 'Yes, Mrs Day, I'll make sure Mummy knows.' Now and then, India caught the bus into town, but these days she worried about leaving Sebastian alone with Mummy for long, and it was a lot of trouble taking him with her round the shops. He whined, and he was too small to carry things.

It was also starting to worry India that they were running

out of money. She collected her mother's widow's pension from the post office each week. The post office was next to the village shop, so India went to them one after the other. Pick up the pension, buy some stamps and cigarettes for Cindy, milk for Sebastian and bread and potatoes. Put some money by for the rent and most of the cash was gone. Sometimes her mother would open her purse and stare at it, bemused.

India found her own solutions. First, she spent the money in her own money box. Then she raided Sebastian's – he never spent his money or even counted it so he wouldn't know the difference. Then she began to steal things from the shop. Small things at first, to cheer her mother up: a ribbon, a packet of hairpins, coloured chalks for Sebastian. And then, when the money really ran out, things to eat. She was very careful and never took anything big or obvious, and always waited until Mrs Day's back was turned to serve another customer or slice a piece of cheese.

Spring came. Their mother seemed to get better. She walked in the garden, carefully, because of her bones. You could see her veins through the translucent skin on her stick wrists. After supper, India put 'My Funny Valentine' on the record player and her mother smiled and told her she was a good girl and let India have a sip of her sherry. Outside, the leaves on the trees unfurled and the blackbirds sang, and the green shoots of the bluebells pressed up through the dark earth in the woods.

Chapter Four

Riley found Pearl in the back garden. She was heavily made-up, with bright red lipstick and black lines along her upper eyelids, and she was wearing shorts and a flowered top that tied at the back of the neck, the sort of outfit Riley associated with beaches and sunbathing. The gramophone was on and music was playing, and a bottle of something was bobbing in a bucket of water.

There was a man sitting in a deckchair. Riley didn't recognize him, but he was young enough to have a spray of scarlet pimples across his face. He was wearing a brown shop coat open over a shirt and trousers and he was holding a glass in his hand.

Pearl said, 'Where *were* you?'

'Working. What's going on, Pearl?'

'Gerry and me were dancing. We've been having fun, haven't we, darling?' Her voice slurred.

Riley lifted the needle off the record and the music died. Then he nodded to the man in the deckchair. 'Who's this?'

'Gerry works at the greengrocer's. He helped me carry my bags home.'

Riley said to Gerry, 'I should push off, if I were you.'

The youth put down his glass and hurried away.

'Spoilsport,' said Pearl. Her eyes narrowed into pale green slits.

'Where's Annie?' he said.

'Annie?' She looked round vaguely.

A moment's fear. Had she left Annie standing outside the school? Or on a bus, perhaps? Or in the greengrocer's shop where she had found Gerry?

'I remember,' said Pearl. 'She's having tea at Linda's.'

Riley felt a wash of relief. He glanced at his watch. 'I'll go and pick her up.'

As he headed back into the house, he heard her say sourly, 'It's easy for you, isn't it? If you were seeing someone else, how would I know? You'd just tell me you were working overtime and I wouldn't have a clue.'

Slowly, he turned back to her. 'I'm not seeing anyone else.'

'Why should I believe you?'

'That's up to you, Pearl.' His gaze locked on to hers. 'But if you like, I'll tell you what I was doing. In the morning, I checked witness statements connected with an arson attempt. In the afternoon, I interviewed a murder suspect.

161

He claims that he was drinking with his brother when I think he was strangling his ex-girlfriend in an alleyway – but then, I think both brothers are lying. In fact, I'm certain of it, and I intend to dig deep enough until I can prove it. You see, I don't believe either of them. They're volatile, they act on impulse and they fly off the handle. They're known for it in the pubs of Deptford. And you can't trust people like that, can you?'

Before her eyes dipped down, he saw the fear in them. 'Stop it,' she muttered. 'Stop it, John.'

He said curtly, 'I'm going to get Annie.'

As he walked back through the house and let himself out of the front door, he unclenched his fists, flexing his fingers. At that moment he felt nothing at all for her, not even pity, and if it had not been for Annie, he would simply have walked away.

A steel-grey sky clamped down the windless air and a cold snap made people dig their warm jackets back out of their wardrobes. March when it should have been June. Old men coughed at bus stops and films of coal dust veiled the leaves of the shrubs. If you ran your fingertips along railings, they came away blackish-yellow.

As Ellen was getting ready to leave the lab one evening, Professor Malik asked her to come to his office.

'You've been with us a year now, haven't you, Ellen?' he said, as she shut the door behind her.

She saw him run his fingers over a piece of paper on his

162

desk. He was frowning; she felt a ripple of apprehension. There were conversations that started like this, weren't there, and went on to include phrases such as, *I hope you can find some other niche more suited to your abilities*, or, *I regret that things have not worked out as I would have hoped.*

She said, 'I hope my work's satisfactory, Professor.'

'Very much so.' The frown deepened. 'Indeed, that's the problem.'

'I don't understand.'

'Sit down, please, Ellen. Your work is exemplary. You are quick and thorough and methodical. In fact, you are an asset to the hospital and I'm sure you will go on to have a long and successful career here, if you so choose. So this confuses me.' His thin brown fingers tapped the piece of paper again.

'What is it?'

'It's the letter that Marcus Pharoah wrote to me last year when I contacted him to tell him that I was considering you for the post here.'

She had been dismissed from Gildersleve without references. She said, 'I told you at the interview, Professor, that I was sacked from Gildersleve Hall.'

'I know you did. You told me that Pharoah didn't think you were suitable for the position and believed you would do better elsewhere. But I wanted to know Pharoah's side of the story.'

It still stung. Pharoah had discounted her as inferior, not worthy of Gildersleve Hall.

Professor Malik went on, 'When Dr Pharoah dismissed you, did he make any specific criticism of your work?'

'No.'

'Are you sure?'

'Completely. I remember every word of our conversation. You don't forget something like that. There was no specific criticism. Only the implication that I was second-rate.'

'I can see no sign of that.'

Ellen felt a surge of relief and pleasure. It was as if a load had been lifted from her shoulders. 'Thank you, Professor,' she said. 'That means a lot to me.'

'I wondered whether to bring up the subject with you. But I felt I had to.'

'I take it Dr Pharoah's comments were uncomplimentary?'

'I wouldn't say that.' Dr Malik turned the piece of paper round so that she could read it, adding quietly, 'I would say they were vituperative.'

Ellen began to read. The first time she read the typed paragraph, she couldn't take it in, so she tried again. Words pulsed like exploding stars, jarring and jabbing sickeningly. *Slovenly . . . incompetent . . . neligent.* And, most woundingly, *If she had spent less time flirting with the male staff her work would doubtless have benefited.*

Aware of a tightness in her throat, she said, 'This isn't true.'

'No, I came to the conclusion that it wasn't some time ago.'

Hateful to think that he had read that. She heard Malik

164

say, 'This doesn't correspond to my estimation of you at all. As I said, your work is exemplary. So unless you had some specific difficulty with what you were doing at Gildersleve Hall—'

'I don't believe so.'

'I'm sorry if this upsets you, Ellen, but I felt you should know that it exists.'

'It doesn't upset me.' She met his gaze. 'You read it, and yet you still gave me a chance. Why?'

'I'm a great believer in second chances.' His smile reached his tired brown eyes. 'I've had a few myself, in the past. You performed well during the interview and I've always preferred to trust my own judgement. Fortunately, I know your supervisor at Bristol personally, so I spoke to him, and he was able to give me a very different view of your abilities. I will admit that I kept an eye on you until I had confidence in your work.' He paused, then added, 'Pharoah is capable of being vindictive.'

'You know him?'

'We've met. We didn't get on.'

Standing up, she held out her hand to him. 'Thank you for telling me this,' she said. 'Thank you for believing in me.'

Leaving the hospital, Pharoah's damning phrases repeated themselves in her memory over and over again. *Miss Kingsley's approach to her work was slovenly, her technique incompetent and her methodology frequently misjudged. If she had spent less time flirting with the male staff, her work would doubtless have benefited.* Coldly, analytically, she surveyed her three months at Gildersleve Hall, and thought, no, none of that is true.

But any employer, reading those comments, would have crossed her off his shortlist immediately. Only Professor Malik's acquaintance with her supervisor at Bristol and the dislike of Marcus Pharoah that he had implied had enabled her to find work at all. Without that turn of fortune, what would she be doing now? Living at home with her parents. Taking some job, any job, and perhaps giving up on science for ever.

No wonder it had taken her six months to find another post, if Dr Pharoah had responded in such a manner to the inquiries of other prospective employers. She might have gone through her entire life believing that it was her poor performance at interviews that was preventing her from finding work, or a shortage of available posts, or a prejudice against female scientists. Time would have passed and soon she would have had a gap on her CV that could not be respectably filled, an open sore that could not be covered over with any acceptable explanation.

Why had Pharoah done it? Why bother? She hadn't mattered. If he had honestly not thought her suitable for Gildersleve Hall, then why not write some bland words that would rid him of her and yet allow her to continue her career? What he had done smacked of spite and contempt. It was never comfortable to find yourself the object of someone else's dislike and she could not remember it ever happening to her before. Such deceit, such treachery.

Marcus Pharoah had wanted to hurt her. He had meant to destroy her. Why?

She remembered her conversation with Alec Hunter, as they had walked together down the drive at Gildersleve Hall. 'Be careful, Ellen,' he had warned her. And then, 'Pharoah has his pets and it doesn't do to say no to him.' How right he had been.

Once, during that Gildersleve autumn of 1952, she had been to a meeting at one of the London colleges and had happened to mention to an acquaintance that she was working at the hall. *So you're at Marcus Pharoah's little fiefdom,* her friend had said. Looking back, she saw how appropriate that term had been. A word from Pharoah and they had all jumped. Impossible to imagine him at a loss or feeling guilty or ashamed of himself. Only once during her time at Gildersleve Hall had he seemed to falter. *I had such ambition then, such vision,* he had said to her in the hotel bar in Cambridge. But perhaps even those words, so apparently out of character, had been an act, designed to elicit attention and sympathy. It seemed to Ellen now that everything Pharoah had done had been with calculation. You fell under his spell and so you didn't notice. It was only afterwards, when you reflected on what had happened, that you saw this was true.

She remembered how the atmosphere had changed whenever he had come into the common room, and how the tension had ratcheted up when he had been nearby. Gildersleve Hall, with its aura of exclusivity and privilege, could not have existed without Pharoah. He had created it, nurtured it, financed it and controlled it. He controlled his staff, too, every bit as precisely as he controlled the hall — through his charm and humour, yes, but also through his unpredictability, and, when it suited him, his capacity to intimidate. Pharoah was used to having his own way. From the eminent war hero, Jan Kaminski, to young researchers like Andrée and Martin, they had all run errands for him and had leapt to do his bidding.

Ellen recalled the quarrels she had overheard between Pharoah and Dr Redmond. Redmond, who had cared nothing for the opinion of other people, had been the only person openly to disagree with Pharoah. Had anyone else dared to cross him, Pharoah would surely have taken them in the palm of his hand and crushed them. She knew this: he had done it to her.

She could not go home yet, she needed to think. Passing an open café she slipped inside, bought a cup of coffee at the counter and sat down at a table by the window. A spray of sugar speckled the cheap plastic tablecloth and the girl sitting opposite her — perm, short-sighted pale blue eyes a few inches from a paperback — glanced at her and then went back to her book.

Ellen ran her hand over the condensation on the window, making a fan shape. Passers-by blurred behind the glass. She cast her mind back to her own involvement with Marcus Pharoah. The lunch at his house, the drink at the hotel in Cambridge. The dinner invitation she had refused and the cooling-off she had sensed after that refusal. *You could have a promising future at Gildersleve*, he had said to her that evening in the hotel. What had made him alter his opinion of her during those few short weeks?

In telling Inspector Riley about the quarrel she had overheard between Pharoah and Redmond she had made a conscious decision not to be one of Pharoah's men. She could not have demonstrated her independence of mind more clearly. Had Pharoah been punishing her for that? Had he seen what she had done as an act of disloyalty?

But was disloyalty enough? You might dismiss someone for their perceived lack of allegiance, but would you set out to wreck their career? Sitting in the café, stirring her coffee, her doubts about the death of Dr Redmond resurfaced. Dr Redmond's threat, the searching of the cottage, the coincidence – and convenience to Pharoah – of his death. It wasn't that she didn't believe in the possibility of coincidence, but her instinct as a scientist told her to reach for it as an explanation only after every other avenue had been explored and dismissed. So far as she knew, she had been the only person at Gildersleve to have questioned the assumption that the death had been accidental. Well, maybe it had been. But something niggled at her; it always had.

She found herself remembering her cycle ride from Copfield to Gildersleve, how the wind had blown the red and gold leaves from the hazels and how she had breathed in the sharp cool air as she had biked down the slope. Her mind had never felt so clear; sometimes, since, she had stumbled through a fog. In her memory, the two events, her dismissal and the discovery that Alec Hunter was still in love with Andrée Fournier were inextricably entwined. Pharoah's condemnation or that embrace, seen from the window of her lab – which had been more painful to her? In cutting off all contact with everyone she had known at Gildersleve Hall, what had she been trying to escape? The shame of her dismissal or the shame of her unreciprocated feelings for Alec Hunter?

The girl with the perm waved to someone outside the window, closed her book and left the table. She had a choice, Ellen thought. She could forget it, put it behind her, get on with the rest of her life. She might even, if she continued to work hard, be able to revive her stalled career. The bruises were beginning to heal and Professor Malik had given her a second chance.

But the scars ran deep, and besides, she would not be allowed to forget Gildersleve Hall or, indeed, Marcus Pharoah himself. Switch on the radio and you heard his voice, opining on the relationship between science and the arts. Open up *The Times* and you saw his name on the byline of an article. And at the end of the column, a footnote: Dr Pharoah is the director of Gildersleve Hall. Dr Pharoah is on the governing board of this or that institution.

They should add another sentence, she thought: *Dr Pharoah destroys careers with the dash of a pen.*

* * *

170

At six o'clock one July morning, Riley co-ordinated a series of raids on half a dozen north London properties suspected of being used to store stolen goods. The operation was a success, the suspects were rounded up, and Riley's super-intendent, an austere, quiet man, murmured approval.

It was almost eight o'clock in the evening by the time the last of the interviews were completed and the final charges drawn up. Driving home to Tufnell Park, Riley had to wind down the car window to stop himself yawning.

He let himself into the house, put his briefcase in the hall, took off his jacket and loosened his tie. He noticed the difference immediately: the quietness of the house – no radio, no gramophone, no clattering of pots and pans in the kitchen.

He put his head round the sitting room door. He didn't see her at first, and then he did, huddled in an armchair in a shadowy corner of the room, her knees drawn up, her head bowed. Riley crossed the room to her and Pearl raised her head slowly, as if it had become unbearably heavy. A glance in her eyes told him that the febrile vivacity of recent months had been wiped away, like a cloth drawn across a blackboard, revealing only darkness.

He said gently, 'Pearl, what is it? What's wrong?'

She was wearing an old cotton dress and no make-up. Her hair straggled round her face and in her eyes he saw confusion. 'I have to stop thinking,' she whispered. 'Make me stop thinking! Please, John!'

He touched her hand. In spite of the warmth of the

summer day, it felt cold and clammy. 'What do you mean?' he said carefully. 'What is it you don't want to think about?'

She made a slow and visible effort to form a response. 'I have these thoughts in my head. They just go on and on.' She licked dry lips. 'I have to buy more milk or I have to remember that Annie needs to take her plimsolls to school and my mind says it over and over again – plimsolls, plimsolls, plimsolls. I hate it. It wears me out.'

She was biting at a knuckle; he drew her hand away, saying, 'Don't, Pearl, please, you'll hurt yourself.'

'And there are the bad thoughts,' she muttered.

'What bad thoughts?'

'About you. About even Annie, sometimes. You'd hate me if I told you.' She closed her eyes. 'I see the way you look at me. I'm not a fool.'

There was nothing he could say. After a silence, she began to speak again, her voice a thready whisper.

'I'm running and running and I can't stop and I can't get anywhere either. And now and then I feel myself falling, and it's a very dark hole and I'm slipping into it, and if I keep on running maybe I'll stay out of it. I'm afraid, John. I'd rather keep on running than fall into that dark hole again.'

He cupped his hands round her face, so that she looked at him. 'Look, I'm going to go and check on Annie. And then I'll make you a cup of tea and we'll talk, and we'll try and decide what best to do.'

'I don't want to talk. I don't want to think any more.' She looked exhausted. 'I wish — I wish I could just stop *being*! I wish I could just — not be here any more!'

Annie was still awake. Her pyjama buttons were done up wrongly and her hair was still in plaits. Riley guessed that she had put herself to bed. He hugged her and sorted her out, then tucked her in and went downstairs to the kitchen and made tea.

Then he went back to the sitting room. He put the cup of tea in Pearl's hands and waited until she had drunk a few mouthfuls. He said, 'I think you'd better go and see the doctor. She'll be able to give you something that'll make you feel better.'

She looked alarmed. 'I hate those pills! I don't need them! I've been fine, most of the time, you know I have!'

'Just for a while,' he said firmly. 'Just to help you through this bad patch.'

'Oh John.' The tea sloshed into the saucer; he took it from her and she buried her head in his shoulder. 'I'm sorry,' she murmured. 'I'm so sorry.'

Dr Ellis wrote a prescription for Pearl 'to tide her over' and said that she would make an appointment for her to see Mr Morris, a psychiatrist. Pearl looked frightened and Dr Ellis explained that Mr Morris was the expert in this type of case. This type of case? What type of case? With Pearl sitting beside him, Riley didn't feel he could ask.

A week later, they went to see Mr Morris. Mr Morris

preferred to speak to his patients alone, so Riley sat for an hour in the waiting room, leafing through old copies of *Horse and Hound*. When Pearl came out, Mr Morris – imposing, pinstripes, fiftyish – boomed, 'Make your next appointment with my receptionist, Mrs Riley,' and beckoned to Riley. Then he lowered his voice. 'We may have to consider hospitalization if your wife's condition does not improve,' he said. 'We shall have to keep an eye on her.'

They went away on holiday for a week to Devon, where a reduced, dampened-down Pearl sat on a deckchair while Annie played on the beach. When they returned to London, Pearl's mother, Vera, stayed over to help with Annie and the house.

Gradually, Pearl improved. The spark flickered, and she started seeing her friends again. Vera went home to Weybridge and Pearl acted out to Riley some of her conversations with Mr Morris, mimicking his mannerisms. She didn't talk about leaving London any more, though sometimes he saw her standing in the garden, smoking a cigarette, gazing over the fence, a hungry expression in her eyes, as if she was searching for something.

Always afterwards, he remembered the weather. It was one of those disappointing late August days, the sky grey instead of blue and a sharp wind blowing, as if the year couldn't wait to turn to autumn. Before he left for work, Pearl told him that Basil was picking up Annie that morning. She had a dental appointment at ten and was getting her hair done in the afternoon, so it was easier for Annie to go to her grandparents for the day. Riley was to collect her after work from his in-laws. Vera and Basil were going to a party that evening at the golf club.

Driving to Weybridge, the traffic was heavy. Friday night, people heading off for their weekends in the country. It was almost seven by the time Riley arrived at his in-laws'. A nice house, detached, surrounded by lawns and flower beds. He parked on the drive and Basil, who was watering plants, came to meet him.

'Hello, John,' he said. 'This is a surprise.'

Riley was confused. 'Why? Have you changed your mind? Aren't you going out?'

'Going out?'

'To the golf club. Pearl said you had something on at the golf club.'

Basil shook his head. 'Not tonight. You've got the wrong end of the stick, old son. But come in and have a drink.'

Riley said, 'But you've got Annie?'

'No.'

'Pearl told me you were taking Annie for the day.'

He saw then in Basil's eyes something that mirrorred his own unease. Basil said, 'I'll go and check with Vera. Don't say anything, John. No point upsetting her.' He strode into the house. Riley followed him.

Vera was in the kitchen, wiping immaculate surfaces. Basil said, 'John's in a bit of a muddle. He thought Pearl had arranged for us to take Annie today.'

Vera looked up. 'No, Pearl said she was taking her

175

shopping.' Her gaze darted between the two men. 'Why? What's happened?'

'Nothing's happened,' said Basil. 'Everything's fine. As I said, John made a mistake, that's all.'

As they returned outside, Basil said, 'Phone me,' and Riley nodded. On the way back to London, he tried to stop himself thinking, keeping functional only the part of his mind that enabled him to choose the quickest route home. But now and then a picture flashed into his mind. Pearl, lying on their bed. Pearl, wearing the red silk kimono with the dragons on it, eyes closed as if she was sleeping. The dragons, the black sweep of her hair, an empty bottle of pills. *I wish I could stop being. I wish I could just not be here any more.*

Riley parked outside the house and unlocked the front door. He called out Pearl's name as he ran up the stairs.

But she wasn't in the bedroom. And she wasn't in the other bedrooms, or the bathroom. She wasn't in the sitting room or the dining room or the kitchen.

Yet he knew it wasn't right. He saw a movement and went out into the garden, but it was only the branches of a neighbour's tree, soughing in the wind, casting a dappled light on the ground. Back in the house, an envelope on the sitting room mantelpiece caught his eye. Riley tore it open and read the letter inside it.

A Friday night in September, and they were giving a party at the lodging house. People squeezed into rooms and corridors and some of the hardier souls spilled out into the tangled back garden. There was the blue curl of cigarette smoke and Jacques Brel on the record player.

Someone squeezed himself on to the sofa beside Ellen. 'Simon Hacker,' he said, shouting to make himself heard over the chatter and Jacques Brel. He offered her a bowl of peanuts.

'Thanks. I'm Ellen, Joe's sister.'

'I know. I asked someone.'

She had a better look at him. Not bad. Broad shoulders, quite tall. Thirty or so, straight dark hair swept to one side, a round face with brown eyes topped with brows that were raised in a way that seemed to indicate both interest and pleasure. A little thicker round the middle, perhaps, than the sort of man she found herself thinking about, wondering about, on a bus or in a quiet moment in her lunch hour. But not bad.

He fetched two glasses of beer and sat down beside her. He told her he was a chemist, that he had been at the Dyson Perrins Lab in Oxford and had now a junior lectureship at Imperial. They had a mutual acquaintance; he named one of Ellen's Bristol friends. Then, shuffling himself round to face her, he said, 'So you were at Gildersleve Hall.'

'I left quite a while ago,' she said. Her usual response to such remarks.

'Can't blame you. Rats leaving a sinking ship.'

'What do you mean?'

'When did you leave?'

'Nearly two years ago.'

'All change since you were there, then.' He had the satisfied air of someone imparting startling news.

Ellen sensed exaggeration, but was interested. Simon Hacker took another draught of beer and wiped his mouth with the back of his hand. 'You'd have been there in Kaminski's time, I suppose?'

Which implied, she thought, that Jan Kaminski wasn't at Gildersleve Hall any more. Which *was* interesting.

'Le Fou du Roi' came to a rousing conclusion. Simon said, 'Cambridge offered him a fellowship. Everyone thought he'd stay at Gildersleve Hall for life. My goodness, Kaminski and Pharoah were almost *married*. Loads of the others have left too. Toby Dorner, but then Harvard's been after him for years. That pretty Frenchwoman. And the Scot, tall fellow, whatsisname, is at King's now.'

King's. Ellen's heart pounded. 'Alec Hunter, you mean?'

'That's the chap.' Simon Hacker drained his glass. 'Would you like to dance?'

They went into the kitchen. Rosemary Clooney was singing something bittersweet, and Ellen let herself be taken into Simon Hacker's embrace. So: Alec Hunter was in London, but that didn't matter because all that had been a long, long time ago, and Alec and Andrée Fournier must be married now, and didn't the bad-tempered pair of them deserve each other. It made no difference to her whether Alec was in Cambridgeshire or London or Timbuktu. And Simon Hacker's hand was running up and down her back, rather as if he were rubbing creases out of her dress, but never mind because she knew that at some point in the evening he'd ask her out to the cinema or for supper. And though she hadn't yet made up her mind what she would say, it would be nice to be asked.

India came into the room. Joe followed after her, with a moony expression on his face. Joe, you idiot, thought Ellen, then looked away, closed her eyes and let her head sink on to Simon Hacker's shoulder.

That autumn, India had decided to be more like Ellen. Ellen would never have got into the sort of mess she herself had, owing people money and being pursued by men she disliked. Ellen had a few mannerisms – that slight raising of the eyebrows when someone said something silly or did something unreasonable, and a quickness of movement as she went about her day-to-day life, as if every moment must be used well. India tried them on, like a new coat, walking a little faster, snapping her handbag efficiently shut like Ellen did. When she found herself getting bored or her mind wandering, she tried to mentally order herself back to attention. She knew how easily you could let things drift. You lay on your bed, leafing through a magazine and listening to 'My Funny Valentine', while around you, abysses opened.

Ellen was one of those people who did more or less the same thing at particular times of the day – eating, going to work, sleeping – but India's life had never been like that. She tried, but events seemed to fling themselves at her, making her do things she hadn't planned to do. Just now, she was trying very hard to arrive at work punctually each day, but it was difficult. She would be about to leave the flat in the morning when a friend would phone, or, because she had been out late the night before, she would pull the blankets over her head when Sebastian brought her a cup of tea and fall asleep again. Or she would wake up in some unexpected bed on the other side of London, with none of her belongings to hand and having forgotten to put a comb in her bag. Miss Maloney, the manager of the art supplies shop, had recently spoken to her about her timekeeping. India had found this lowering: she loved her job and didn't want to lose it. And yet she had detected a certain resignation in herself, a sense that such things were beyond her control. She had expressed this thought once to Ellen, but Ellen had been dismissive of it. 'It's up to you, India,' she had said. 'You can make your life into whatever you want.' Things were very cut and dried in Ellen's world.

India and Ellen were sitting in Ellen's bedroom, eating biscuits and drinking cocoa. Ellen was talking about her boyfriend, Simon Hacker, with whom she had been going out for some weeks. He had a motorbike, on which Ellen rode pillion to cafés or the cinema, where they watched French films. 'He has nice eyes,' said Ellen, 'and we talk about interesting things.'

India had introduced Ellen to some of her more respectable friends and some of them had fallen in love with her, but it had never gone any further than silent admiration.

They found Ellen daunting – too aloof, too brainy, too serious, too beautiful. India had often wondered how on earth it was that so many couples managed to marry. One so rarely met a man who did for everything. One man might be nice to go to dinner with, another might be fun in bed, and yet another might have money, and so on. But eventually the man for going to dinner with would let slip that he had a wife and children in Acton, and the man with the money would reveal a habit of counting every penny in his pocket and begrudge her even a chocolate bar. Or, like Garrett, he might be handsome and charming and funny, but feckless and unreliable too. Miss Maloney might say that she, India, was unreliable, but Garrett was worse. He had a habit of going off for weeks at a time without even sending her a postcard and she had more than once sat in a bar for hours, waiting for him, only to end up having a drink with a complete stranger instead.

India asked Ellen whether Simon Hacker was in love with her, and Ellen looked alarmed, from which India deduced that he might be, but that Ellen wasn't in love with him. India sympathized. There was something about a man telling you he was in love with you that made you notice his faults. Almost as if, by declaring himself to be the sort of man capable of falling in love with you, he showed his poor taste, so that adoration in itself made him undesirable.

Eventually, Ellen stopped talking about Simon Hacker.

India suggested they go and see *The Barefoot Contessa* the following evening but Ellen said that she couldn't because she was going to a lecture. 'I'll come with you,' said India. Ellen said no, it was a scientific lecture, someone she knew was giving it and India would only be bored. India was offended and Ellen, seeing that, sighed. 'Yes, all right then,' she said. 'If you really want to.'

But she *was* bored. The Royal Institution was in a very grand building in Albemarle Street and for a while India enjoyed just looking at it. The exterior was adorned with massive pillars and inside there was marble flooring and echoing corridors. India had never been in a lecture theatre before. The rows of seats were steeply raked; above them a balcony contained yet more seats. All this to listen to a man rattling on by himself for an hour.

It was at first like watching a play: the sense of anticipation, the ripple of interest as the lecturer appeared from the wings, then the applause followed by a sudden silence. India sat still, having promised Ellen she wouldn't fidget. The lecturer, who was tall and dark and film-star good-looking, distracted her for a few moments. He had a nice voice – a Bournville chocolate voice, Peachey would have called it.

But soon the silence and the murmur of the speaker's voice began to send her into an irritated stupor. She noticed every itch, every crease in her clothing. She wriggled, tugging down her skirt, hitching up a stocking. Ellen's eyebrows rose and India tried once more to sit still. She moved surreptitiously, so as not to disturb Ellen again, and scratched her leg.

The lecturer was talking about diseases, something to do with blood. India tried to concentrate, but couldn't make head or tail of what he was saying, and besides, the phrase 'bad blood' had lodged in her mind and stayed there. Could blood be bad? Could some dark taint run through it, staining your character, marking you apart? And if so, didn't that mean that you were stuck with how you were? There was luck, wasn't there, and there were the cards you were born with. Could you make yourself into a different person, as Ellen seemed to believe, or did the dark blood that ran through your veins mean that you had no choice but to submit to whatever events were thrown at you?

At last, from the floor of the lecture theatre, there was a bang and a puff of smoke and everyone clapped. Another man stepped forward and made a short speech, thanking the speaker, and then said, 'The floor is now open for questions.' Ellen was sitting on the edge of her seat, leaning forward, and India thought she might raise her hand to ask a question, but she didn't. The questions, which weren't at all interesting, seemed to go on for ever and India had to bite her lip to stifle a yawn.

Eventually, to her immense relief, there were more thanks, another round of applause, and the audience began to shuffle to their feet.

Ellen said, 'Wait here, India. I'll be back in a moment. Don't move,' and hurried down the central aisle.

India picked up her handbag, stood up and adjusted her frock (black moiré silk with a white angora bolero) and followed Ellen down the steps. Ellen was standing to one side as a group of people huddled round the lecturer. A very fat man with an almost completely bald head spoke to India. He said how interesting the talk had been. 'Dr Pharoah is such a marvellous speaker,' and India said politely, 'Yes, isn't he?' though it had been deadly dull.

Ellen was talking to the lecturer, Dr Pharoah. India went to join her. Ellen gave India a cross look – guiltily, India recalled being told to sit still.

The lecturer said, 'Aren't you going to introduce me to your friend?' and Ellen said, rather snappily, 'India, this is Dr Pharoah. Dr Pharoah, this is Miss Mayhew.' Then a voice called out, 'Ellen! How are you? Haven't seen you for ages, thought you'd emigrated!' and she turned away, looking flustered.

Dr Pharoah said to India, 'What field are you in, Miss Mayhew?'

'I wouldn't say I was in a field exactly.'

'Then you have an interest in the heritability of disease?'

'No, none at all.'

He laughed. 'If you're telling me you were bored, I'll be mortified.'

He was very handsome, quite old, and far too sure of himself. 'I was terribly bored,' she said. 'I almost fell asleep.'

He didn't look mortified at all. 'Then I shall have to remember to talk to you about something else next time we meet.'

'Oh, I doubt if that'll be necessary,' she said. 'I shouldn't think we move in the same circles at all. Good evening, Dr Pharoah.' And as she walked up the stairs of the lecture theatre, India knew that he was watching her.

One Friday evening, Ellen worked late at the hospital to help Professor Malik get through the rush. She had noticed that since their conversation about Dr Pharoah, he had encouraged her to take on more challenging tasks, running some of the tests on her own.

It was eight o'clock before her work was complete and she was able to go home. Taking with her a sheaf of results that the professor had asked her to drop off, she left the lab. She handed in the papers to Sister Casualty and walked out through the Outpatients' Hall. The hospital, and the steps that led up to the front doors, was busy, Friday night bringing its customary collection of victims of drink-induced accidents and fights.

She was making her way down the front steps when a man in navy-blue overalls staggered, stumbling against her. Knocked off balance, she put out a hand to save herself, dropping her briefcase and handbag. She caught a gust of beery breath as the man slurred curses.

A voice said sharply, 'Watch what you're doing!' and a hand reached out to her, steadying her as she fell.

Blue overalls' companion muttered, 'Ted, you lummox,' adding, 'Sorry, miss, he's had a few too many,' as he hauled his friend through the doors of the hospital. Ellen found herself sitting in an undignified manner on the steps, among the sweet wrappings and cigarette ends, holding a stranger's hand.

No, not a stranger. A voice said, 'Hello, Ellen. Are you all right?' and she looked up and recognized Inspector Riley.

He helped her to her feet. Ellen tugged at her skirt and dusted herself down. 'Yes, fine, thank you – oh no, my things!'

Her briefcase had fallen open and a cold, nagging breeze was gusting papers down the steps, strewing them like litter over the threadbare patches of lawn. As they ran around, chasing them, she expressed her surprise at meeting him here, and he explained that two of his colleagues had been injured in a car accident that afternoon, and that he had been visiting them.

When everything was gathered together again, Riley said, 'There's a café over the road. May I buy you a coffee?'

As they walked away from the hospital, she found herself looking at him, reminding herself of him. Tall, with features that were classic, almost severe, he had a kind of restrained handsomeness. A second glance beneath the flare of a street lamp allowed her to see that he looked fatigued, shadows round his eyes and a tightness to the jaw.

He said, as they crossed the road, 'How are you, Ellen? Are you well?'

'Very, thank you.' She explained, 'I work at St Stephen's.'

They entered the café. While Riley went to the counter, Ellen inspected the damage. There was a graze on her knee and, more annoyingly, a hole in her stocking, put on new only that morning. She stacked her papers into some sort of order, put them back in her briefcase and rubbed the grime off her handbag. The espresso machine hissed and gurgled and her gaze moved to where Riley stood at the counter. He had a knack of coming across her in situations that were hardly to her advantage – shocked and scratched after she had discovered Dr Redmond's body, or hurled to the ground by a drunk.

He carried the coffees to the table and sat down. She smiled at him. 'Nothing's missing and only my pride is damaged. Thank you for your help.'

His hand waved away her comment, and his eyes, with their light flickering of green and brown and gold, settled on her. 'So you decided to leave Gildersleve Hall?'

Her mood, which had lifted on seeing him, darkened. 'I didn't *leave*,' she said bluntly. 'I was sacked.'

'Sacked? I'm sorry to hear it. When was that?'

She wondered whether he was revising his estimate of her, remoulding her into the sort of woman who couldn't hold down a job. 'Nearly two years ago,' she said, adding, to spare him the calculations, 'A few weeks after Dr Redmond died.' And, finding that she did not want him to think badly of her, she explained, 'I think Dr Pharoah was angry with me for telling you about his quarrel with Dr Redmond. He told me that wasn't so, but I do believe it.'

She realized that at last she could think about what had happened without shame – and that, she supposed, was something. She told Riley about Dr Pharoah's lecture at the Royal Institution. 'I managed to speak to him when the lecture was finished,' she said. 'He'd written such unpleasant things about me to my professor at the hospital, you see, and I wanted to know why.'

'What did he say?'

'That it had been his true estimation of me at the time. That he was sorry I found my dismissal so hard to accept that I needed to invent fanciful explanations for it. And that I needed to reassess my opinion of my own abilities.'

Riley raised his eyebrows. 'Whew.'

'Quite,' she said grimly. 'I couldn't even think of anything crushing to say in response.'

'One never can at the time.' He smiled at her. 'One always thinks of just the right thing as one walks away.'

'It doesn't matter now. I enjoy my work at the hospital. And I'm loving being in London.'

Checking her watch and seeing with a sinking feeling that she was already late meeting Simon, Ellen apologized and explained that she must head off. They left the café together, she heading for the Underground station, Riley to where his car was parked.

She asked him where he was living now.

'Tufnell Park,' he said.

'And your wife – and you have a daughter, don't you? How are they?'

'Annie's very well.' Something crossed his face; she saw him look about. Then his gaze fell back towards her, unreadable and guarded, and he said, 'Pearl left me three months ago. I haven't seen her since and I've no idea where she is. I've enjoyed meeting you again, Ellen. Take care of yourself.'

Then he walked away from her, in the direction of King's Cross, and was soon lost among the crowds on the pavements.

Ellen and Simon had been going out for more than two months, long enough to get to know each other. They shared some interests, and he was a kind and well-meaning man, but she had found herself noticing certain habits of his: a tendency to fuss about his health and to talk about himself at length, as well as a way of telling anecdotes, his narratives so stretched out and pounded into submission that whatever event he was describing lost any capacity to amuse. She knew that she must break off the relationship, but so far her attempts to do so had come up against the solid wall of Simon's adoration. It was hard tactfully to part from a man who was telling you that you were the best thing that had happened to him for years. She must face up to the fact that tact – and kindness, too, if necessary – must go by the board: she must be firm tonight, and put an end to it.

Sitting on the Underground train, Ellen's thoughts turned to Riley. She was aware that she had talked largely about herself during their brief conversation – perhaps she was catching it from Simon – and yet something terrible and heartbreaking had recently happened to him. His wife had left him, and he had implied that she had also left their daughter. How did you survive something like that? She had found mere dismissal from a job almost too much to bear, and so her heart ached for him. He seemed to her a serious man, intelligent and perceptive and, she suspected, capable of deep feeling, so how would he cope with the absence of a much-loved wife? Had he friends, had he family? Or did he, like so many men, bottle up his emotions?

She knew that she had always been so fortunate in her family. Tightly-knit and united, they were always there for her. She couldn't recall ever having heard a word of criticism from either of her parents, and though Joe might tease her, she had no doubt that he would also have gone to the end of the world for her if she had needed it, as she would have done for him.

She could see clearly the effect that family break-up had on a person whenever she spent time with India and Sebastian. That lack of a solid rock, that absence of anything certain to grasp on to showed through in India's impetuosity – even, perhaps, in her need to take whatever she took a liking too. Ellen could not have said she knew Sebastian well – he was too shy, too wary to permit intimacy. India had hinted at an illness after Sebastian had been